THE
MAGICAL
BOOKSHOP

THE
MAGICAL
BOOKSHOP

KATJA FRIXE

Illustrated by
FLORENTINE PRECHTEL

Translated by
RUTH AHMEDZAI KEMP

ROCK THE BOAT

A Rock the Boat Book

First published by Rock the Boat,
an imprint of Oneworld Publications, 2021

Originally published in German under the title *Der zauberhafte
Wunschbuchladen* by Katja Frixe with illustrations by Florentine Prechtel.
© Dressler Verlag, Hamburg 2016
Published by agreement with Dressler Verlag, Hamburg, Germany.
English translation copyright © Ruth Ahmedzai Kemp, 2020

ISBN 978-1-78607-566-6 (Paperback)
eISBN 978-1-78607-567-3

The translation of this work
was supported by a grant from
the Goethe-Institut.

GOETHE
INSTITUT

Printed and bound in Great Britain by Clays Ltd, Elcograf S.p.A.

Oneworld Publications
10 Bloomsbury Street, London,
WC1B 3SR, England

MIX
Paper from
responsible sources
FSC® C018072

For Vera,
who lives far too far away,
and yet is always here with me

CONTENTS

1

THE WORLD'S WORST DISASTER

If your best friend tells you that she's moving away, it is time for Red Alert. Absolute state of emergency. What can you do? You urgently need to come up with a way to prevent it. And it might be that you have to do things that are a teeny tiny bit forbidden. The kind of things that make grown-ups press their hands against their faces in despair or furrow their brows, or both at the same time.

And that's why, on the day my dearest friend Lottie was supposed to get on the train and move away to a new town with her mum, I wanted to make sure she disappeared. I mean Lottie, not her mum. Lottie had of course agreed to this plan of action and had helped me with the preparations. We also had two accomplices. Not the shifty kind that you get in gangster movies.

No, our accomplices were far more refined, or perhaps we should say a bit more unusual – because they were a rhyming cat and a talking mirror.

Gustaf the cat and Mr King the mirror lived in Mrs Owl's Bookshop, and that was exactly where I planned to hide Lottie.

The plan was actually quite simple. Mrs Owl arrived every morning at eight o'clock on her bright green bicycle, with Gustaf the cat perched in the front basket. First, she opened up the shop, let Gustaf in and then went next door to Chocolate Heaven to get some chocolate brownies for breakfast.

Lottie and I planned to use this opportunity to scamper into the bookshop and hide. Fortunately it was still the summer holidays and luckily, no one seemed to have noticed that we had sneaked out of the house at a very un-holiday-like time of day.

"But Clara, what if we get caught?" Lottie asked for about the hundredth time since I had told her the plan. We were huddled together behind the smelly bins near the entrance to Mrs Owl's shop.

"That's not going to happen," I whispered back for about the hundredth time, even though I wasn't really sure myself. "At least not right away. We're going to hide you, and then when your parents look for you, they'll talk to each other and finally realise that maybe they need to think about you, not just themselves."

This was the problem, you see. Lottie's parents weren't speaking to each other and hadn't done since her dad fell in love with another woman. I could understand that Lottie's mum was furious and that she didn't want to live here any more, in our small town where they constantly bumped into each other. But moving a hundred miles away and taking Lottie with her? That simply wasn't acceptable.

"I hope it works," said Lottie.

I squeezed her hand to give us both courage.

"Look – she's coming!"

My heart started pounding as Mrs Owl leaned her bike against the tree in front of her shop.

Gustaf, who was sitting as always in the little basket on the handlebars, craned his black-and-grey stripy neck to peer around attentively. When he spotted us, he quickly looked the other way.

Lottie and I held our breath as Mrs Owl opened the bookshop door with a whistle, let Gustaf in and headed back out for Chocolate Heaven.

Phew – so far, so good.

Mr King often scolded Mrs Owl for leaving the shop open for every Tom, Dick and Harry to come in and steal the books, but then she always just stroked his thick gold frame and said, "My dearest mirror, books cannot be stolen. They always come back to their owner."

4

And most of the time this reassured Mr King.

As soon as Mrs Owl disappeared into the cake shop, Lottie and I leaped out of our hiding place.

"I'll keep watch," cried Mr King as we stormed into the bookshop and dashed upstairs to the children's books section.

Gustaf leaped after us, chattering away excitedly. "I can't believe what I'm seeing," he mewed. "It's like a thriller with you two fleeing!"

Lottie was the first to reach the small staircase and she climbed at lightning speed up to the mezzanine level. This cosy corner overlooking the rest of the shop, with its wooden floorboards and handrail, was the children's realm, and for Lottie and me there was no better place in the world. We spent whole days lounging around on the comfy beanbags, reading our favourite books. But there would be no browsing today – I had to make sure of that.

"Lie flat on your tummy at the back," I whispered, and Lottie pressed herself against the floorboards, just as we had discussed yesterday. I pushed two beanbags in front of her until she was completely hidden from view.

"Is that OK?" I asked Gustaf, who was now standing at the shop door, looking up in our direction with his green eyes.

"For all I stare and all I know, not even a strand of hair on show!" he confirmed. "Perfect!"

"Are you OK, Lottie?" I asked.

The response was a muffled "*hmpf*", which I interpreted as "yes".

A weight lifted from my heart, because the first part of our mission was complete. Now Lottie just had to stay undetected until her parents started looking for her – together!

I dashed down the steps from the mezzanine level. And not a second too early.

"Attention, Mrs Owl's coming in to land!" Mr King's voice boomed through the shop, so I quickly dropped down onto the beanbag at the foot of the staircase, grabbed a book and pretended to read.

Gustaf jumped into his usual spot, a green armchair in front of the poetry shelves, curled up and closed his eyes. "I'll curl up in this heap and pretend to be asleep," he hissed, before the door opened with a loud tinkle of the bell.

"Good morning," chimed Mrs Owl, as she walked into the shop carrying a large paper bag from Chocolate Heaven. She flung her shoes into a corner, for there was nothing Mrs Owl liked better than walking around barefoot.

Although I hadn't made a sound, her gaze drifted straight towards me. "Clara!" she called out, a cheerful smile spreading across her face. "Couldn't you sleep? Or...What else would drive you out of the house so early in the holidays?" She held her nose in the air and sniffed. "Mmm, what's that interesting smell?"

For a moment I was afraid Mrs Owl would sniff out Lottie's presence, because it was the sort of thing I could imagine her being able to do. But then I smelled it too. It was a bit like cinnamon and tangerines.

"Ah, I think I know where that's coming from," said Mrs Owl, no longer interested in my answer to her question. She put the bag down on the counter and walked with determined steps over to the shelf of cookery books. She ran her nose along the row of books until she finally stopped in front of a thin volume. "I knew it!" She pulled out the slender book and addressed it sternly. "We'll be opening in an hour – then you can start showing off. I'm sure someone will buy you straight away. But for now, please pull yourself together," she said, placing the book back on the shelf. "If all of you cookery books start pumping out your aromas, people will think they're in a restaurant, not a bookshop."

I no longer found it unusual that Mrs Owl spoke to the books. Or that the books suddenly began to smell or draw attention to themselves in other mysterious ways. This was just how things worked in Mrs Owl's Bookshop.

Mrs Owl had a knack for finding the perfect book for every customer, before they even realised what it was they were looking for. As soon as you came into the shop, she had an incredible ability to sense precisely what mood you were in. She could always tell straight off if someone was in a good mood or bad, happy or sad. She also had help from Mr King, whose years of experience of reflecting people meant he could see inside people's innermost thoughts and even reveal what didn't show on the outside.

Now Mrs Owl turned back towards me. "So, your world's a bit topsy-turvy today, is it?"

I could feel myself blushing – could she tell from looking at me that I had something to hide? That I had helped Lottie hide up on the mezzanine?

"N-no," I stuttered. "Everything's fine."

"That was my idea," Mr King intervened. "Clara looked rather tired, so I suggested she reads a book upside down, to stimulate the brain cells and revive the spirit."

Only now did I notice that the writing in the book I was holding was upside down.

"That's right," I agreed. "Thank you, Mr King! I feel much more awake and invigorated than five minutes ago."

I nodded at the mirror, whom I hadn't yet had a chance to say hello to properly. Mr King was a grand mirror about two metres high and a metre wide, with a thick gold frame. He had the best position in the shop because, leaning against the wall opposite the front door, he was always the first to see who came into the shop.

"Ah, well, that's good to know, Clara!" said Mrs Owl. She leaned over the counter and reached towards the till with her index finger. "And what are *you* doing here? Shoo! Back in your book!"

I saw a small yellow butterfly excitedly flap its wings as Mrs Owl gently pushed it on to her palm.

"How are people going to notice your wonderful book if there's just a blank front cover?"

Mrs Owl went over to one of the bookshelves and blew the butterfly from the palm of her hand back on to its book.

Then she shook her head. "Funny. What's going on today? What has happened that has got all the books so excited?"

She let her gaze wander thoughtfully through the shop, and I felt my hands get hot and sweaty from nerves, sure that our cover would be blown and the plan would be over before it had even started.

"I've got it, I've got it!" Gustaf yelled suddenly.

Mrs Owl stopped looking around and walked over to the green chair. I silently thanked the cat for distracting her.

"I thought you were asleep," said Mrs Owl, laughing, and she sat down beside him.

"Yes," he mewed. "But I was dreaming about how I could become famous and rich, and that was when I awoke with a twitch."

"And how are you going to do that?" Mr King asked in a sullen voice.

"I shall write a book. What do you think of that? *Gustaf's Verse for Better or Worse* – a title well suited to a rhyming cat."

"Couldn't you think of a duller title?" muttered the mirror.

"Why, I can make anything rhyme, please don't give me strife! While you are stuck in one place, I lead a fulfilling life."

I couldn't resist a grin. Gustaf and Mr King bickered constantly.

Mrs Owl got up, clapped her hands and declared, "That's quite enough of the squabbling! As you know..." and here we all joined in, "...today's no day to be down in the dumps!" She often said this to cheer us up, and it was true – you could hardly be down in the dumps for long when you were in her shop, even today, with Lottie hiding from her imminent move.

I'm not sure whether it was because of Mrs Owl or the colourful characters she shared her shop with or the countless books – it was hard to say – but whatever the reason, the bookshop was my absolute favourite place in the world. It wasn't far from our house, and I probably spent more time there than with my family – my parents, my two brothers, Jacob and Finn, and my grandma. My grandma told me recently that the bookshop and Mrs Owl were there when she was my age – ten and three-quarters – but Dad says that's non-sense and Grandma is starting to lose her marbles. He probably thinks she must be wrong because Mrs Owl doesn't look any older than Mum.

Mrs Owl had long, dark blonde hair, which she usually had tied up in a slightly scruffy bun. She had green eyes surrounded by lots of little wrinkles, a nose that was rather large for her face and a mouth that was always laughing – or smiling at least. She often wore green dresses because dresses are so comfortable, and green is her favourite colour.

But as young as Mrs Owl looked, it was possible that Grandma was right. Because in Mrs Owl's bookshop, time didn't seem to work in the same way as anywhere else. Today, for example, time passed by very slowly. It seemed to me that Lottie had been in her hiding place on the mezzanine for hours, but in fact it was just twenty minutes. But it also happened the other way around. Sometimes, when I thought I'd only been flicking through books for a few minutes, I would look out of the shop window and find it was already dark.

Mrs Owl disappeared into her office and came straight back out with a tray. On it were two plates with a chocolate brownie each. "One for you and the other…" she said, winking at me. "Just in case."

I didn't even want to imagine what she meant by that. Instead I got up from the beanbag and walked past the fully laden shelves to the counter. The shop almost had the feel of a living room belonging to a very well-read old lady who had an unbelievable number of books. And yet Mrs Owl always knew exactly where every book was. And if she did ever lose one, she could be sure that it wouldn't be long before it caught her eye.

In the middle of the shop were two tables where Mrs Owl laid out a range of her new favourites each month, and this month they were all about France. She had guidebooks, novels by French authors and recipes for French cuisine. And to set the right musical atmosphere, she had been playing CDs of French *chansons*. Amid all the books there were always a couple of green "eye-catchers" (as Mrs Owl called them): the lamps,

Gustaf's armchair, where he liked to doze off when there wasn't much happening in the shop, and the beanbags in the children's area and downstairs under the mezzanine.

Mrs Owl picked up a stack of books and started to put them on the shelf next to the till. "Here," she said, holding one out to show me. "Wouldn't that be a good one for Lottie?"

I flinched when Mrs Owl mentioned Lottie's name and then stared at the blurb of the book without really reading it. "Yes," I said. "Right. Can I take it with me when I say goodbye to her later?" I gulped. *Oh, please, don't let it come to that.*

"It's not going to be easy to say goodbye, is it?" Mrs Owl peered at me with her green eyes, as if searching right inside my head for an answer.

"Aaaaaaaaatchoo!" Gustaf's sneeze was unnaturally loud for extra effect, but this time Mrs Owl didn't let herself be distracted by him. She kept her eyes fixed on me.

I was just about to say something when the shop door flew open and in rushed a customer, who seemed to be in a hurry. Everyone in the neighbourhood knew that Mrs Owl wasn't very strict about her opening hours and you could sometimes pop in a little earlier.

When I turned around, I realised that unfortunately it wasn't a normal customer: it was my dad. He was wearing his slippers and pyjamas, and on his head he had the embarrassing *I love Dad* baseball cap that my older brother Finn had bought him during an exchange trip to the USA last year.

"Clara!" Dad shouted, rushing towards me. "There you are! Why aren't you asleep in bed? And what's with the note? 'Don't worry'?" He stamped his foot. "Of *course* I was worried! And so were Mum and Grandma and..."

"I'm sorry, Dad," I said, and I really did feel a bit remorseful. "I couldn't sleep and I didn't have anything to read, so I came to see Mrs Owl."

Dad pulled me towards him for a hug with one arm and with the other hand he reached for a chocolate brownie that disappeared straight into his mouth.

"And where's Lottie?" he asked sternly.

"No idea!" I said. "How should I know?"

"Well," Dad said, pretending to think hard, "perhaps

because she's your best friend? And because, just like you, she also vanished from her bed *before 7a.m.* – suspiciously early for the summer holidays! – which we know because her mum called us. And because Lottie happened to leave exactly the same note as you."

Oh no. Lottie's mum wasn't supposed to call my house – she was supposed to call Lottie's dad!

"I-I..." I stammered, biting my lip. I heard a thud up above.

Hearing the noise, my father spun around to see where it was coming from. "What's that crazy cat doing?"

Gustaf had jumped to the top of the poetry shelf and was trying to push a book out with his paw. "Finally the fruit of my endeavour. I've searched for this book since forever!" he said, but only Mrs Owl and I could hear him.

That was another funny thing about this shop. There was a talking cat and a talking mirror, but only Mrs Owl and I could hear them – nobody else, not even Lottie. I had no idea why that was the case, but every time I asked Mrs Owl, she just responded with another question: "Why do you need to know?

Would it change anything?" I didn't have an answer to that, so at some point I stopped asking and only wondered about it occasionally when I was lying in bed at night.

"The cat is looking for a good book for you, Mr Jacobsen," said Mrs Owl gently, passing Dad a poetry book and the other chocolate brownie. "Here, one for the road – I presume you haven't had breakfast yet. Perhaps you could tell Lottie's mum that it might be best to follow Lottie's advice. Life is so much easier if we worry a bit less, isn't it?"

"That's true." Dad nodded and stared at the poetry book. "But isn't Lottie...?" He looked around doubtfully.

"Can you see Lottie here?" asked Mrs Owl.

Dad shook his head. "No, I can't," he said, almost convinced.

I tried not to look up at the mezzanine level. *Please, Lottie*, I thought, *don't sneeze or cough or make any noise!*

Mrs Owl also remained focused. She clapped her hands, making the small, glittering pendants jangle on her silver bracelet.

"It's probably best to go home now," she told my father. "We'll let you know as soon as we hear from Lottie. All right?"

I didn't know where to look, I had such a guilty conscience. Everyone was worried about Lottie and there I was just keeping quiet.

But we didn't come up with this plan to annoy our parents. Lottie's dad was to blame for this mess. And his new girlfriend. So I just stared at the floor defiantly as Dad left the shop.

"Phew," said Gustaf. "That went well."

Mrs Owl put her arm around me and sighed. "Well, I'd better pop next door again," she said, picking up her bag. "I've got a feeling we're going to need some more of those little chocolate brownies. And in the meantime," she said, looking at Mr King, Gustaf and finally me, "why don't you go and let Lottie out of her hiding place?"

2

CHOCOLATE CAKES AND BEST FRIENDS

It was twenty minutes before Mrs Owl returned from Chocolate Heaven, and the reason for that now balanced on a huge plate before us: chocolate brownies, chocolate biscuits, chocolate muffins, cream-filled chocolate rolls, rocky roads dipped in chocolate, custard-filled chocolate doughnuts, chocolate chip cookies. It looked like Mrs Owl had cleared out the entire shop. The plate was now on the children's mezzanine, and Mrs Owl, Lottie, Gustaf and I were sitting around it. Mrs Owl had been quick to scribble, *Closed — back soon* on a piece of paper which she hung on the door before coming up to join us.

"I should have known that you would want to spend your last day together in your own special way," she said with a smile.

Lottie looked like she had just seen a ghost, she was so pale. Apart from a brief "Finally!" when I freed her from her hiding place, she hadn't uttered a word.

Of course we'd known that our game of hide-and-seek wouldn't last long, but now it was clear that our plan hadn't worked out at all as we had hoped. There was no going back. My best friend was going to have to get on the train with her mum in a few hours and we both knew we wouldn't see each other for a long time. I'd often read about people with heartache and had always wondered what that felt like. Now I was pretty sure I knew. Having to say goodbye to your best friend feels like a broken heart. Maybe it's even worse. It makes you feel very heavy, like your heart isn't beating properly any more, and you're just infinitely sad.

"I would have liked to have had a nice farewell party for you," said Mrs Owl. "With colourful bunting and balloons and chocolate cake and...well, a touch of melancholy, but also lots of good cheer."

She carefully lifted the plate and held it in front of us. "But we're fine with just chocolate and a touch of melancholy, right?"

Lottie and I stared at the mountain of chocolate on the plate but something prevented us from reaching for one of those delicious mouthfuls. Perhaps we were afraid of destroying the moment and unwittingly pressing an invisible button that would make the clock start ticking towards 4:30p.m., when Lottie's train would roll out of the station.

But someone didn't seem to share this concern. Gustaf stood on his hind legs to get a better view of the plateful of cakes, craning his neck so far forward that he lost his balance and landed with his nose in a chocolate cream bun.

Lottie started to giggle, and it was so contagious that I couldn't help joining her. Gustaf turned to glare at us and tried to lick the cream off his face, which was when I really exploded with laughter. I fell back on to the beanbag and held my stomach. Lottie flopped on to the beanbag next to me with a snort of laughter and wiped away two or three tears – I don't know if they were from laughing or whether she had just started to cry before that. In any case, we were snorting, grunting and wheezing with laughter, and by the time we calmed down we were exhausted and probably both thinking the same thing: how good it was to have a best friend and how much we were going to miss each other.

Meanwhile, Gustaf had licked off every last speck of cream; all that remained on his face was a grin. "See! That's how a cat can come in handy. *Gustaf wrestles with food and picks up your mood!* Now will you take a seat and have something to eat?"

Lottie and I let our eyes wander over the plate again and then both reached for a rocky road.

"You first!" we both said at the same time, and then we had to laugh again.

"Sometimes we have to reach the peak of sadness before we can rush down the mountain and open our eyes to what's beautiful around us," said Mrs Owl.

She did have a funny way of expressing herself sometimes, but I could sort of see what she meant. I didn't know what life would be like without Lottie. The town that she and her mum were moving to was an hour and a half away by train. We would be able to visit, of course, but that was completely different from seeing each other every day and walking to school together. School without Lottie – that was like Mrs Owl's shop without Gustaf and Mr King.

After we had polished off almost everything on the plate, Mrs Owl got up and clapped her hands.

"Well, girls, it's time," she said. "We had better take Lottie home now."

"Can't I stay for a tiny bit longer?" Lottie asked. "It's still a while before our train leaves."

"But your mum is worried," said Mrs Owl. "And I'm sure there are still a few things left to do." She started climbing down the rickety steps. "Come on! I have another surprise for you!"

A grin spread across Lottie's face. "I love surprises!" she squealed, and we followed her down.

"Stand in front of Mr King," said Mrs Owl.

"Oh, what an honour," the mirror gasped.

I looked at Mrs Owl with a raised eyebrow. Lottie didn't know what she was planning either.

"In front of Mr King?"

Mrs Owl nodded and gave a knowing smile.

Lottie and I exchanged looks, then both shrugged

and stood in front of the mirror, arms hanging at our sides.

"Like this?" I asked.

"No, no, no!" Gustaf cried indignantly. "Gustaf enjoys a little more poise."

Mrs Owl gave us a meaningful wink. "I want you to know, girls, that what you see in the mirror is the image that will remain with you both."

I don't know if there were ever two best friends more different than us, but with the exception of our haircuts, there wasn't really anything about us that was alike: my eyes were green, Lottie's were brown; Lottie wore glasses, I didn't; Lottie had dark hair, mine was blonde; Lottie was a bit shorter than me and loved bright colours like pink and yellow, while I would happily wear my dark blue sweater with little silver stars every day.

"Should we do something?" Lottie asked Mrs Owl.

She just shrugged and said, "That's up to you. It's your picture!"

I still didn't really know what she meant. Lottie was quicker than me to realise and she put her arm around me and pretended to kiss me on the cheek. She made me giggle and I hugged her tight, pulling a funny grimace.

"Much better," murmured Mr King, satisfied.

Then I started squinting and sticking out my tongue, and we carried on pulling silly faces and poses, jumping up and down until we eventually ended up on the floor, in fits of laughter.

Gustaf and Mr King were also laughing, which Lottie couldn't hear, of course.

"I think you're ready to say goodbye now," said Mrs Owl, helping us up. "And until you next see each other, you'll both have this."

She handed each of us a book, with a picture of two girls fooling around on the cover, pulling a silly pose with their hands on their knees and their mouths gaping open with laughter, while a yellow butterfly fluttered between them. These girls were Lottie and me, just as we'd looked a moment ago in the mirror. Lottie looked at Mrs Owl in surprise, but I had long stopped asking her how she did it, how it was that the books gave off smells, how bits of them could float around the shop, or why only I could hear Gustaf and Mr King speaking. In Mrs Owl's Bookshop these things simply happened.

I opened the book and saw nothing but blank pages.

"These are two very special friendship books," said Mrs Owl. "Use them to write to each other – about what you're doing, how you feel, what thoughts are going through your mind. I promise you that your friend will be at your side when you're writing in your book." Mrs Owl put one arm around me and the other around Lottie and hugged us close. "You'll soon be physically separated but in your hearts you'll be as close as ever."

Mrs Owl always had the best ideas.

"Thank you," I said, stroking the photo on the front cover.

Lottie gulped. "Thank you. I'm sure this will make it easier."

I hoped Lottie was right. I would try it out that very evening.

Three hours later, I was standing on the platform with Mum, staring at the train as it rolled out of the station, carrying away my very best friend and taking her to a new life without me.

"I'm so sorry, darling," Mum said helplessly, squeezing my hand.

She had taken time off work to come with me to the train station, which was quite unusual, because my mum only ever allowed herself a day off when one of us was really ill. She worked in a law firm and always had a lot to do.

"It will get better," she said. "Believe me."

"When can I visit Lottie?" I asked.

"Well, let's give her a while to settle into her new place, OK? Then we'll talk about it."

I tried to swallow the lump in my throat. The train snaked across the tracks and almost vanished into the distance.

"Your friendship is very special," said Mum, "because you two are both very special." She kissed my forehead. "And you always will be."

I snuggled up to her and breathed in her very special Mum smell, which, no matter what, always made me feel like everything was going to be OK.

Mum stroked my head. "There's not really anything I can say to make it better, Clara. Your best friend has moved away and that's really, really rubbish. It's completely and utterly...pants!"

I freed myself from our hug and looked at her

in surprise. Mum rarely said bad words in front of us, but I'd never heard her call something "pants" before!

"Yes, you heard right," she went on. "It's just…pants. And that's why…" she said, with a brighter expression on her face, "you can choose whatever you want to do today. I've got the whole afternoon off, and we can do whatever you feel like."

Now I was torn. I knew how much it meant for Mum to take a day off work, and I loved that she had made time for me. But all I really wanted to do was go back to the bookshop, curl up in one of the beanbags with a book and forget everything around me. I knew that was the best distraction, so that's what I told Mum.

She gave me a puzzled look. "No ice cream? Or swimming?"

I shook my head. "Maybe at the weekend? I don't feel like it today."

Mum thought for a moment. "OK," she said finally with a smile. "Would it be all right then if I drop you off at Mrs Owl's, pick up a book and leave you there for a bit?"

"Fine with me," I said, giving her one more squeeze.

Ten minutes later, we were back at the bookshop and Mrs Owl was greeting us as if it was forever since she'd last seen us.

"*Oh la la*, it's so wonderful to see you!" she said, giving Mum a conspiratorial wink. "There are two magical books I've been waiting to show you." A dull thud suggested that these two books had just flung themselves off the shelf. "Do come and see," Mrs Owl sang, taking Mum's hand and leading her to the back room of the shop.

That was all right by me, as I could disappear up on to the mezzanine and make a start on the book Mrs Owl had left out for me earlier, as if she'd known I'd be back.

I snuggled into a beanbag, ran my hand across the smooth front cover of the book and took a deep breath. Mrs Owl's Bookshop was the only place you got this distinctive mix of book scent (I had no other name for it), coffee (Mrs Owl drank it by the gallon) and fresh flowers (there was always a bouquet in a vase by the till). I opened the book and began to read. Mrs Owl had an amazing talent for picking out stories that immediately had me gripped. The room around me faded away and with it the cheerful hum of my mum and Mrs Owl chatting. I didn't even think about the sad departure of my best friend. For a while, at least.

It was only when the bell on the shop door rang and I heard a loud "Byeeeee!" that I resurfaced from the book and saw my mum stepping out of the shop.

"Nothing like the perfect literary find to get things off your mind?" Gustaf called up to me from down by the shop window.

"Absolutely," I said. "Mrs Owl has sniffed out another good one!"

"Easy to sniff when it has a good whiff," Gustaf rhymed with a snigger. "Another rhyme for that book of mine."

"Other people work quietly and don't disturb others in the process," grumbled Mr King, but when Mrs Owl clapped her hands he fell silent.

While Gustaf paced back and forth by the window, looking out for customers, I suddenly found I could no longer concentrate on the words in front of me. I couldn't help thinking about Lottie again, wondering how I was going to survive the first day of school without her. It was just two days away. The thought of it made me want to hide in the corner and crawl inside a book!

The first day of school after the summer holidays was usually one of my favourite days of the year. Everyone was in a good mood and excited to see each other again, full of stories about where they had been and what they had been up to over the holidays. Lottie and I always loved spotting changes in the other students, like who suddenly had spots or a new haircut. There was always something new about someone in the class. But this time I wouldn't have anyone whispering in my ear, no one to eat with at break time (Lottie always had Nutella sandwiches and I always had liverwurst) and no one to vent to when Vivi and Sarah wound me up.

I put down the book and climbed down the rope ladder. "None of this would have happened if it hadn't been for Lottie's idiotic dad Daniel meeting that stupid Sophie Rose," I grumbled.

Sophie Rose
was the name of the woman Lottie's dad
had fallen in love with. The reason Lottie's mum decided to move away. I had only seen her once, but once
was enough. I saw her walking arm in arm through the
park with Lottie's dad and she had this ridiculous way
of throwing her head back when she laughed. Ugh,
what a poser!

"Sophie Rose...hold your nose...everyone knows...
she's got smelly toes!" rhymed Gustaf, and I had to laugh.

"It's true!" I said, running my fingers along a row of
books, then sitting down in Gustaf's green chair. "She's
a genuine stinker, that Smelly Toes Sophie Rose!"

Mr King cleared his throat. "Pipe down, you two,"
he said. "Customers approaching."

The shop door opened.

"*The books await, the clock ticks...and here are customers five and six!*" Gustaf shouted excitedly and sat down
in front of Mr King.

"Hey, out of the way!" the mirror complained.
"You're blocking my view!"

34

"Will you two stop arguing?" I exclaimed from where I was sitting, clapping my hands like Mrs Owl had earlier.

Suddenly, everyone was as quiet as a mouse, and I had that feeling like when you're called up to the front of the class to answer a question and you don't know what to say. As if everyone's staring at you. My gaze wandered to the shop door. And my face flushed hot and red, because there in the doorway stood Vivi and Sarah.

If Lottie was my absolute best friend, then Vivi was my absolute worst enemy. She was the meanest girl I knew. And no matter what you did, Vivi always managed to find ways to be meaner still. She was, of course, always super sweet and polite to the teachers and to Sarah, who always did exactly what Vivi told her to do.

"Who were you talking to?" asked Vivi with a sneer, glancing around the shop. "There's nobody here!"

Unfortunately, Mrs Owl had just disappeared into her office at that moment.

"Were you talking to yourself?" giggled Sarah as she gave Vivi a friendly nudge. "Must be because Lottie's gone. She's got no one left to prattle to."

"Yeah," Vivi said. "No one to talk to except books!" She laughed a spiteful laugh.

"Ugh, who are these cackling crows?" Gustaf asked. In his horror he had even forgotten to rhyme.

I sank deeper into the chair. I felt my throat tighten and I couldn't for the life of me think of a good comeback. Gustaf snuggled up against my legs and suddenly, out of nowhere, Mrs Owl was standing next to me.

"Can I help you?" she asked Vivi and Sarah. Her voice sounded friendly but at the same time quite stern.

Even Vivi was suddenly, unusually sheepish. "Have you got the new one in the *Holly Polly's Perfect Pony* series?" she squeaked.

Mrs Owl smiled. "No, I'm sorry. I've just sold the last copy. She whinnied with joy as she galloped out of the shop."

I had to suppress a giggle.

"*Pfft*," Vivi snorted, grabbing Sarah by the sleeve and turning around. "Then we'll buy it somewhere else!"

"Goodbye. I hope we don't see you again!" called out Mr King.

Gustaf added, "Off you go, you cackling crows."

Mrs Owl closed the door behind them. Then she snorted. "*Holly Polly's Perfect Pony*. There is more to reading than pony books, you know!"

All I could do was force a strained smile as it dawned on me that Vivi and Sarah would be off gossiping about me, telling everyone I spent my spare time talking to books. My first day of school without Lottie was going to be a disaster.

3

POTATO PANCAKES MAKE
EVERYTHING BETTER

I wasn't exactly in the best mood when I got home – even if my nose was aware of an enticing smell. Someone had been frying potato pancakes and that someone was probably Grandma. She knew that potato pancakes were my absolute favourite food and I'd be sitting down at the kitchen table in no time. Today was different though, because I wasn't hungry at all. In fact, I was actually feeling a bit sick. Probably because of all the chocolate earlier and, of course, because I was feeling down about Lottie. Besides, I was annoyed. Annoyed with Vivi and Sarah for being so horrible and annoyed with myself for not being able to think of anything mean to say back to them. Why did I even care what they went around saying about me?

Mrs Owl had given me a new book that I really wanted to go and read. It looked like it was going to be funny: on the cover was a cat floating in space in an astronaut suit. That was the sort of pick-me-up I needed right now.

But I hadn't factored in my family. No sooner had I hung up my jacket on the peg than my little brother Jacob came charging towards me.

"Clara!" he shouted. "We've turned the living room into a cinema! There's popcorn and snacks, but you have to hurry – the film's about to start!" He handed me a piece of paper that I presumed was supposed to be a ticket. "And you can have Dad's chair! That's the best seat! Don't you want to know what film it is?" he prattled on, not stopping for a breath. "*Rescue Raffi!* Raffi's a hamster and..."

"Sounds great," I said, smiling, because it was just so

sweet and touching to see how excited Jacob was, and how much trouble he and Dad had gone to. I thought for a moment. I could always go and sit in my room and read the book later; I'd better not miss the chance for this one-off film night. And who knows, maybe it would be an even better distraction than reading.

"I'll just get changed into something comfier, OK?" I said, ruffling Jacob's hair.

"Yeah, yeah, yeah!" Jacob shouted and ran back to the living room, where he jumped up and down enthusiastically in front of the television. "She said yes!"

Dad came into the hall with the remote control in his hand and winked at me. "You've made a little man very happy. And a big one too. Glad you're joining us."

When I came downstairs, Mum was standing at the bottom of the stairs. "Well, how was Mrs Owl?" she asked. "Did she manage to cheer you up?"

"Yeah, kind of," I said. "But I think the main Cheer-Up-Clara event is yet to start!" I nodded towards the living room.

Mum smiled. "Have you eaten yet? I asked Grandma to make potato pancakes today."

She looked at me as if she had just told me I could

have a pony for Christmas (which, by the way, wasn't on my wish list; Lottie and I both wanted new inline skates). Because while I loved potato pancakes more than anything in the world, for Mum there was nothing more disgusting.

"I'm not hungry," I said, but I felt really bad that Grandma was slaving away in the kitchen to make me happy and I'd just disappeared into the living room to watch a film without even saying hi.

"Come on," Mum said. "At least go in and say hello. She's also worried about you."

"OK," I said, even though I knew that Grandma wouldn't stand for any "I'm not hungry" business.

"Close the door – it's draughty!" she barked from somewhere amid a dense cloud of smoke.

From Grandma's greeting it didn't sound like she was particularly worried about me.

"Why don't you turn on the fan?" I asked, trying to wave the smoke away from my eyes.

Grandma pushed open the window and suddenly the air in the kitchen cleared. "The fan, *pfff*!" she said. "Podge's sensitive ears can't stand the noise."

Podge was Grandma's dog and he almost never left

her side. His name wasn't actually Podge – it was Arco – but when he started getting fatter and fatter, Finn gave him his new nickname. Podge ignored me, but lay on the floor beside the stove, panting and hoping that something would fall on the floor for him. He was such a pig that he would even go for raw potatoes or eggshells.

"Sit down, darling," said Grandma, waving her spatula. "Your favourite food is the best thing for grief. Always has been."

I sighed because I didn't have the heart to tell her that I had no appetite.

"Darling, that won't be the last time in your life that you have to say goodbye. Best get used to it."

Grandma never minced her words. Maybe it was because she had already been through a lot in her life – losing Grandpa, for example. She had lived with us ever since he died, which was sometimes good – like when she cooked your favourite food – and sometimes slightly less

good, like when she told you what she thought straight to your face.

Grandma slid a thick lump of margarine into the pan and dropped in three dollops of potato batter. Then she brought over a plate with a mountain of already cooked pancakes on it. "Here, help yourself before the rest of the pack piles in."

As soon as she said that, the door opened and my big brother Finn shuffled in. He raised a limp hand in greeting. "You can use my computer if you want. To chat or whatever."

I looked at him in surprise. Finn had spoken to me? Not just one word, but two sentences? This was unheard of. Normally you didn't see him all day and he wouldn't emerge from his room until the evening when everyone else was already in bed. And now he was also offering to let me use his sacred computer!

But suddenly I understood. Mum must have told everyone that they had to be extra nice to me today. I smiled, because that was typical of my family. Everyone always got on with their own thing – Grandma watching her mushy tear-jerkers on the TV, Dad wandering around with his beloved camera, Finn sitting in front of the computer, Jacob building racing-car tracks in his room and Mum working – but whenever one of us was down or having a hard time, we all came together and were there for each other. On the one hand, it was a very nice idea to always have a house full of people who looked out for one another. On the other hand, it also made me a bit sad, because here I was with my parents, my brothers, Grandma and Podge. But Lottie? Lottie had no one in her new home besides her mum. My heart felt heavy again.

"Thanks, Finn!" I said, so softly that he probably didn't hear me. I wanted to say something else, but my brother helped himself to a plate of pancakes, piled it high with apple sauce then disappeared from the kitchen without another word.

Podge waddled over to me and rested his head on my thigh. He looked at me pleadingly, and though he couldn't speak like Gustaf, I knew exactly what he wanted.

But under her grey curly hair Grandma seemed to have eyes in the back of her head because, even without turning around, she hissed, "No potato pancakes for Podge! He'll get fat!" That was pretty funny, because Podge was already bursting at the seams, and that was certainly not my fault. Grandma shared her snacks with him every night when she sat in front of the TV.

Anyway, I shook my head firmly, at which point the pooch trotted back over to Grandma and lay down at her feet.

The potato pancakes in front of me smelled irresistible. All the same, I was sure I couldn't manage a single mouthful. But I didn't want to disappoint Grandma, so I picked up the fork in slow motion and...

"Clara, the film's about to start!" Jacob shouted outside the kitchen door.

Saved!

As if on command, I stood up and gave Grandma a kiss on her wrinkled cheek, which always smelled slightly of peppermint, even here in the smoke-filled kitchen.

"Coming!" I called to Jacob. "Thanks for the potato pancakes, Grandma," I added.

"You're the best potato pancake maker in the world. But first I have to go to the cinema."

Grandma looked at me, unperturbed. "They're best cold anyway," she said as she scooped up a pancake and tossed it to Podge.

"Grandma!" I said reproachfully, shaking my head again, and then went into the living room.

Next to Dad's armchair was a small table with a glass of apple juice, a bag of sweets and a bowl of popcorn. Dad and Jacob really had thought of everything.

"Come on," I said to my little brother as I plopped into the chair, "there's space for two in the best seat."

Jacob snuggled up to me, and I laid Mum's green blanket out over both of us. We were barely twenty minutes into the great hamster adventure before Jacob nodded off. Dad and I still watched the film to the end, then Dad picked Jacob up and carried him to bed.

"Thanks," I whispered, "that was a great idea."

Although I was really tired myself, I had one more thing to do before going to bed (besides brushing my teeth). I went upstairs to my room, switched on the light and sat down at my desk. Then I took Mrs Owl's book out of my bag and gently ran my fingers over the photo of us laughing.

Lottie and Clara. Clara and Lottie.

I paused. Did it feel like Lottie was sitting next to me? Not really. Well...no, not at all. But maybe that was still to come.

I looked out of the window down at the lamplit street. Perhaps Lottie's mum had fallen asleep on the train, and Lottie had seized the opportunity to get out at the next station and sneak on to the first train back. Perhaps she would walk around the corner any second now, as if nothing had happened. I stared into the darkness, but the pavement remained empty. So I grabbed my pen.

Hi, Lottie, I wrote. Nothing. Not even a hint of my best friend.

What had Mrs Owl said? Maybe I just had to write a bit more. But what?

I have no idea what to write, I continued.

That was what Lottie always said in class whenever Mrs Richter set us one of her stupid essay topics. I chewed on my pen for a while and stared at the animal posters on the wall that Lottie always made fun of. But

I loved animals – they were cute – and anyway I had no desire to stick any pop stars up in my room.

Then I just wrote down everything that came into my mind, about our friendship and how we had got to know each other on the first day of school. I told her about Finn's two whole sentences earlier and about Podge, who was about to burst. I was just about to start describing Grandma's watchful eagle eyes when I felt the lightest flutter on my cheek. I carefully reached up and the little butterfly from Mrs Owl's shop landed on my finger.

"Hello, you," I whispered, and as I studied it, I imagined Lottie sitting in her new room surrounded by removal boxes, scribbling away in her book just like me.

At that moment I suddenly understood what Mrs Owl had meant. It really was a bit like Lottie was here with me and I was telling her everything that had happened today.

I forgot that I was tired and sat there writing more and more, and every now and then I let out a loud giggle. It was almost like at school when we passed little scraps of paper back and forth with silly drawings.

I'd filled four pages by the time I was finished – Mrs Richter would have been proud of me! One last good-bye to Lottie, then I closed the book.

I was genuinely relieved. Lottie and I would manage, somehow.

4

A NASTY SURPRISE

And then there it was: the first day of school after the summer holidays. The first day of school without Lottie. Mrs Owl had given me some tips to help me get through the day. She suggested I wear my favourite clothes to help me feel comfortable – ideally something green, of course, because green puts you in a good mood. She'd also had the idea of going to school barefoot – it would make a nice change from all the boring people wearing shoes. But I had the feeling people would probably laugh at me. I had lain awake half the night thinking about Lottie and how she would be feeling about her new school. Unlike Lottie, at least I already knew my classmates, whereas she had to get to know them all from scratch. Poor Lottie.

There was pandemonium in the classroom. I edged through the crowd, trying to get to my seat as inconspicuously as possible. Of course, that didn't work.

"So, Clara, did you say good morning to your books?" whispered Vivi, poking Sarah in the side.

"Naturally!" I replied with a fake grin. "Just not to *Holly Polly's Perfect Pony* – it's a bit too pink for my liking."

Vivi blew her fringe out of her eyes. "Then you probably don't know yet but pink is *in* this season. It just so happens that I was in the USA this summer and *all* the women were wearing pink."

She thought she was particularly cool when she said "You-Ess-Ay". I turned around without another word and dropped into my old seat.

Normally, Lottie and I would have analysed everything together: who had new clothes? Who had been away on holiday and where, and who hadn't and why? Now I had to watch the action alone.

Vivi was entirely kitted out in pink from the "You-Ess-Ay", Clemens now had really weird hair and we had a new classmate: a blond boy with glasses half a head shorter than the other boys, who was just squeezing past Nino and Darius. Grandma would call those two ruffians because they were always picking a fight with other kids, but the new boy probably didn't know that yet.

"Hello, Clara," mumbled Nora, who had got braces during the holidays.

"Hey, did you have a good holiday?" I asked without much energy.

"Yes," she said. "I did an English course in London. There were lots of nice people, and we even had real English tea and biscuits." She smiled as though she were the Queen herself, except with braces.

I thought it was pretty mean of Nora's parents to make her do an English course during the holidays. That would have left no time for the lovely things! Like going to town with your mum or lying in a hammock and gazing up at the bright blue sky or sending a message in a bottle with your best friend or reading from morning till night.

"And you?" Nora asked. "What did you do over the holidays?"

I gulped. For the first few weeks I had spent every

single day with Lottie. We went to the pool in the morning and the bookshop in the afternoon, and she stayed over at mine, either sleeping in the bunk bed or we'd stay in the tent Dad helped us put up in the garden. But I didn't tell Nora that because I was worried I'd get upset.

Instead all I said was: "Reading mostly. I read a lot this summer."

It wasn't a lie.

I started fiddling with the charms on my bracelet. Mrs Owl had given it to me a few years ago for my birthday. She had a similar one – it was silver, and the little dangling charms were set with tiny shards of mirror. Not for the first time, I imagined that my bracelet had magical abilities. If I just rubbed it long enough, perhaps my greatest wish would come true. I narrowed my eyes and rubbed and rubbed and rubbed and imagined that Lottie's dad Daniel would call Lottie's mum Sandra and apologise to her and beg her to come back because he still loved her, and that Sandra would say yes, and that she and Lottie would get on the next train and come back home. At least that's how it was in those schmaltzy TV romances Grandma watched.

And Lottie would call at mine every morning on the way to school and...

"Can I sit here?" a voice asked.

I opened my eyes in confusion. Lottie? Had my wish come true already? But then I saw that the blond new boy with the glasses was standing in front of me and pointing to the chair next to me.

"Darius said it might be free."

I swallowed. That was Lottie's place and nobody else was supposed to sit there. Certainly not a boy! What if

Lottie came back some day? She would be devastated if she saw I'd just found myself someone new to sit next to. I sat up straight and looked around. "There's a space next to Tom. Back there."

I felt almost as mean as Vivi, because the place next to Tom was *always* free because Tom couldn't concentrate if he sat next to someone. But how was the new boy supposed to know that?

The new boy wasn't interested in that seat though. "I'd rather be a bit closer to the front," he said, tapping his glasses. "Blind as a bat, you see."

I had to laugh because I imagined him dangling from the ceiling trying to read a book, every now and then squinting over my shoulder.

"So?" asked the boy.

I didn't know what to do. Did I even have the right to defend Lottie's place? After all, the chances she would come back were pretty slim. But I couldn't be forced to sit next to a complete stranger!

"Is there a problem?" Nino growled from behind me.

He sauntered over and barged straight into the new boy. Then he and Darius were both there in front of my table, standing with their arms crossed and staring at me defiantly. I couldn't remember if they had ever picked a fight with a girl, but I wouldn't put it past them.

But the new boy wasn't rattled in the slightest. "Everything's fine," he answered with a smile. "We're just talking about what we got up to in the holidays."

"Oh, right..." Nino looked a bit disconcerted, because the new boy didn't seem at all intimidated. "OK then," he said finally.

"If you're ever looking for trouble," hissed Darius, "you know where to find me."

Then they disappeared again.

OK, it *was* pretty brave of him to stand up to them. "My name's Clara by the way," I said. "And of course you can sit here."

We'd make the best of it, somehow or other. Maybe he was good at maths, and I could copy his answers, or perhaps his mum gave him a bar of chocolate every morning for break time, which he would share with me.

"Leo," the boy said, putting his bag down beside the table.

"But I have one condition!" I added quickly. "If my best friend comes back, you'll have to sit somewhere else."

"You're like my sister," he said. "There's always a *but*." He carried on in a squeaky voice. "Yes, you can borrow this book, but don't crease the spine! Yes, you can have some chocolate, but you have to give me some gummy bears in exchange. Yes, you can use Dad's computer in a minute, but first I have to send seventeen emails to my friends."

I had to laugh again. "Still," I said, "do you accept my condition?"

He held out his hand and smiled. "Deal!"

I smiled back, but we were interrupted when the bell started ringing and the classroom door opened.

"A wonderful, good morning, everyone!" came a cheerful voice. I looked up and I suddenly felt hot and cold at the same time. Hot with anger and cold with terror.

Our new teacher had long, brown hair and dangly silver earrings. She was wearing a bright red dress with a weird pattern. Her nails were painted red and on one finger sparkled a ring. I had seen this woman before – arm in arm with Lottie's father...

"My name is Sophie Rose and I'm new to the school. And from today I'm your class tutor!"

I stared at her and didn't know how to stop the questions buzzing around in my head.

What's going on? Why is Smelly Toes my teacher? Why is she at my school? How can someone so heartless even become a teacher in the first place? And now what am I supposed to do???

The laughter around the class tore me from my thoughts. Did Smelly Toes crack a joke?

"Did I miss something?" I asked Leo.

He grinned. "Ms Rose told us some of the nicknames her previous students gave her. She said she's sure we won't be able to think of any she hasn't heard before."

"Ah," I said, annoyed that the others found her so funny. Besides, Gustaf would almost certainly come up with lots more names that Hold Your Nose Smelly Toes had never heard before.

Now she started walking around the room carrying a basket full of pens and notebooks covered in glittery paper. "I'd like you all to take a notebook and a pen." When she held the basket under Vivi's nose, she pulled out a shiny pink notebook and ran her fingertips over it as if it were gold.

"Thank you. It's…beautiful!" Vivi whispered, and I wondered why she always had to be so over the top.

"I would be delighted," said Smelly Toes, "if you used your notebook like a journal. Not a secret diary but an open one that others could read. Like me, for example."

Never in my life would I let Smelly Toes read my diary!

She continued, "Write down what you like most about school, what annoys you, any feedback for us teachers, any ideas about what you'd like at school…"

I'd like to see you disappear, I thought bitterly.

"Sometimes it's easier to write things down than to say them directly. So, be brave and use your journal whenever you want."

Now Smelly Toes was in front of me and Leo, and my heart was pounding. I couldn't look at her, so I stared stubbornly at the tabletop. She pushed the basket into my field of vision and I had to admit that the notebooks were really lovely. I almost reached out to take one, but then my eyes fell on Smelly Toes's fingers holding the basket, her red-painted nails, her sparkling ring – almost certainly a present from Lottie's father.

I kept my eyes fixed
on the table and my heart
pounded louder and louder. Then I mustered
up my courage and said, "I don't want one."

It came out of my mouth so quietly and quickly that I wasn't sure Smelly Toes heard me. Which
was probably for the best, because that's not what
you say when someone offers you something. But
on the other hand...

"You don't have to," said Smelly Toes, who had
obviously heard me perfectly well. Her voice was
friendly, and she added, "If you change your mind, just
let me know. I'll keep one aside for you."

The first day at school was even worse than I could
have imagined. It was obvious where I needed to go
as soon as the last bell went: to Mrs Owl's Bookshop.
Because if anyone was going to cheer me up, it was my
friends there.

As soon as I entered the shop, Mrs Owl and Gustaf
were standing in front of me, looking at me expectantly.

"Soooooooo?" they both asked – in unison, as
though they had been practising.

I took off my backpack and dropped it onto Gustaf's chair.

"A total disaster," I said, whereupon Mrs Owl ran behind the counter and brought out a plate with two chocolate tartlets, which she handed to me without saying a word.

Gustaf threw his paws in front of his face in horror and Mr King groaned out loud when I told them about my new teacher. But they didn't seem to think the boy sitting next to me sounded like a problem.

"What exactly bothers you about him?" asked Mr King, interested. "Did he have an unpleasant aroma or was he impudent in his behaviour?"

I had to laugh, because "impudent" was a typical thing for Mr King to say. "No," I said. "He didn't smell bad and there wasn't anything impudent about him."

"Well, then he's a true gentleman!" cried Mr King. "I don't understand why you think negatively of him."

I thought about it. Actually, Leo had been nice and polite and he even made me laugh. Still, I didn't want him sitting next to me.

"Leave her be!" hissed Gustaf, before I could think about it any longer. "She'll have her reasons, you see!

After all, when you think twice, do you find every customer nice?"

"But I've known most of these customers for many, many years. And when someone who I don't know comes in, I peer into their soul."

Mr King did indeed have a deep understanding of human nature, which he sometimes passed off as clairvoyant ability. He had lived in a theatre for years and before that in an antiques shop. So many people had stared at him over the years that he had learned an awful lot about their traits and feelings.

"Just wait and see, Clara," he said. "I suspect the reason you don't want to have anything to do with the boy you now sit next to is because he's not Lottie. But if you can overcome this grief, you might see that he's not such a bad person after all."

We talked more about Leo than about the Smelly Toes problem, which was somehow much, much worse.

"If that stupid stinker ever comes into the shop, have a look into her soul, will you?" I said. I was just about to start up again about how impossible I found her and her behaviour, when both Mrs Owl and Gustaf's faces froze.

I looked over at the shop door, which opened at that very moment.

"Oh no" was my response.

"Here's a whiff of smelly farts: the troublemaker Mr Schwartz," rhymed Gustaf before he jumped up on to my lap.

"Inhale, exhale," said Mrs Owl softly. Then she cheerfully exclaimed, "Mr Schwartz, to what do we owe this pleasure?"

I heard a faint scraping sound at my feet, and as I looked down, a little cartoon devil with a trident ran past me. I put my foot in his way and he glared at me.

"*Pssst*," I hissed, nodding at the bookshelf. "Back on the shelf!"

He raised his trident menacingly then strutted back to the shelf, where he disappeared into a book.

Now I turned to look at the devil in human form who had just entered the shop. Mr Schwartz.

"I've just come to retrieve what is mine," he said in a sinister voice, as he walked towards Mr King.

"Don't touch me!" Mr King shouted, but Mr Schwartz couldn't hear.

"Please don't touch the mirror, Mr Schwartz," said Mrs Owl gently.

Mr Schwartz wasn't deterred and ran his hand over Mr King's gold frame.

"Stop that this instant!" cried Mr King. "Or I won't be held responsible for my actions!"

The antiques dealer looked like a real crook in his dark coat and black hat pulled down over his face. "Soon you'll be mine again!" he whispered. And to Mrs Owl he said, "If you won't give it to me of your own accord then I'll force you to, even if I have to carry it out of here myself."

"*Pah*," exclaimed Gustaf boldly, "you haven't got the muscle or clout to hustle and bustle our old friend out!"

I had to giggle, whereupon Mr Schwartz shot me a vicious glare.

"I'll gladly explain it to you again," said Mrs Owl in her cheerful singsong voice. "You can always buy a book from me." She pulled one off the shelf at random. "This one, for example! But my furnishings are not for sale."

"But the mirror is mine," hissed Mr Schwartz. "Why can't you understand that? If you really want to keep it, then pay me for it! I'd be content with ten thousand euros."

Mrs Owl let out a loud laugh. "Would you like some chocolate cake?" she asked in a particularly soft voice, almost just a sigh. "Something sweet always lifts the spirits! I feel that's something you could benefit from."

Mr Schwartz waved her away then turned towards the shop door. "One day that laughter will be gone!" he said, and he was off.

Mrs Owl sighed and went behind the counter to pop a little chocolate brownie into her mouth.

"Why does he think Mr King is his?" I asked.

"Please, I don't want to be reminded!" moaned Mr King.

"He really did once belong to Mr Schwartz at the antiques shop," explained Mrs Owl. "But that was many, many years ago. Mr Schwartz sold him to the theatre for a lot of money, and when they no longer needed him after the theatre was renovated, he came to me."

"Now Mr Schwartz claims he only lent me to the theatre and that Mrs Owl's purchase wasn't legal," Mr King added. "He's probably hoping to make some

more money from me because his antiques business isn't going so well."

Mrs Owl swallowed the last of her chocolate brownie and then clapped her hands. "Today's no day to be down in the dumps! Certainly not to be down in the dumps about Mr Schwartz! Clara, will you help me sort out a few books?"

"I'd love to," I said, realising that I wasn't nearly so down in the dumps now.

5

A VERY SPECIAL BOOK TIP

When I set off the next morning, my mood was back at rock bottom. I'd wanted to Skype Lottie in the evening and tell her everything about my crazy first day of school, from Smelly Toes and Leo to my afternoon in the bookshop. But Finn seemed to have forgotten his promise about letting me use his computer; that is, he had barricaded himself in his room and wouldn't let me in. So I wrote it all down in the friendship book, but this time I didn't get even a hint of a feeling that Lottie was there with me. The butterfly didn't appear this time either. I imagined the little cartoon devil standing guard with his trident preventing the butterfly from fluttering out of the shop – maybe that was why it hadn't come.

"Hey, out of the way!" I heard a voice behind me, and before I knew it a bicycle sped past.

Darius. And wherever Darius was, Nino couldn't be far behind.

"Don't you have eyes? This is the *bike track*!" he shouted, bashing me with the school bag that hung over his shoulder.

"Idiots," I muttered, but quietly so they wouldn't hear.

"Hey, I heard that," said a voice, but it didn't sound like Darius or Nino.

I turned and quickly jumped on to the pedestrian track in case anyone else was planning to ride into me.

"Why are you walking? You'd get to school much faster by bike," said Leo, as he slowly rode alongside me.

"Don't want to," I said. "Besides, sometimes you bump into someone and then you can chat more easily than on a bike."

Leo looked around. There was no one else on the path. "Makes sense."

He probably thought I was crazy and that I had an invisible imaginary friend. Like Vivi and Sarah, who thought I liked talking to books.

"OK, well, I'll ride on. See you in a bit!" With that, he pedalled off, racing after Nino and Darius.

I sighed. Hmm. Well, at least he resisted making any nasty comments.

I looked at my watch. Still ten minutes until the bell. Perfect – I could stop at the corner shop and buy a top-up card for my phone. I only had it for emergencies, and if I used up the credit for the month, I had to top it up with my pocket money.

In the shop it turned out that I had some credit left. My parents must have realised that Lottie leaving was a mega emergency and topped up my account with a bit of extra credit. So I still had the two euros that Mum had given me for break and decided to invest it in a bag of sweets.

When I left the shop, I popped a sour strawberry in my mouth and quickly texted Lottie:

Walking to school is rubbish without you!

She texted back straight away:

Tell me about it! Have to go by bus and I'm sitting next to a really weird guy.

Like the new boy I have to sit next to now, I typed, when all of a sudden I felt a dull pain on my forehead.

Ouch! That hurt. I looked up and realised I'd walked into a lamp post. It was like something out of a cheesy comedy. How embarrassing. I turned around to make sure no one had seen me. *I hope I don't get a bruise*, I thought as I rubbed my throbbing forehead. That would give Vivi and Sarah yet another reason to tease me. I put my phone back in my pocket so I could get the rest of the way to school without any more accidents.

When I arrived, the playground was deserted. That was funny, because normally it was as busy and noisy as a funfair. I looked at the clock. No! I was late! I should probably have let Mrs Kowalski at the corner shop pick out a selection of sweets for me rather than wondering for ages how many liquorice sweets and how many sour strawberries I should have.

My heart dropped again when I remembered who we had for our first lesson. German with Smelly Toes. Maybe I could quickly call Grandma and ask her to ring the office and let them know I was coming in late. Sometimes she enjoyed playing along, but if I was unlucky, Dad would answer the phone, and then I had to come up with an excuse for why I was calling. So, hmm, not a great idea.

I ran to the second floor where our classroom was. I had to take a deep breath to summon up the courage to knock on the door and open it.

"Clara, there you are!" Smelly Toes called joyfully, waving a wad of worksheets. "We were just about to start."

Didn't she want to know why I was late?

"Leo told us you were stopped," she went on.

I looked at him with a questioning frown, whereupon he just grinned.

"It can take a while to give directions to someone who doesn't know the place," added Smelly Toes with a chuckle. "I remember the first time I got lost in the streets around here...Anyway, sit down and then we can get started."

I dropped my bag on to the floor by the table and flopped on to my chair. "Why did you tell her that?" I whispered.

"So you didn't get in trouble," Leo replied. "Or should I have said that you were just dawdling along? Where have you been all this time?" He pointed a finger at my forehead. "And what happened there? Did you get into a scrap with someone?"

I quickly touched my forehead. It had come up in a lump. Oh, great. How embarrassing.

Smelly Toes cleared her throat for silence, so I spared him a detailed answer. "Thanks," I whispered, then looked down at my worksheet.

A short while later, I felt a vibration in my pocket – that could only be a new message from Lottie. Smelly Toes was walking around between the rows of tables, explaining what we were supposed to be doing. When she had her back to Leo and me, I risked taking a peek at my phone.

Better a weirdo to sit next to than no one at all 😔 Lottie had written.

I felt a huge lump in my throat. Wasn't there anyone in her new class who wanted to sit next to her? *Lottie! Oh, Lottie, I'm so sorry*, I thought, and that was exactly what I wanted to write next. I was just starting to type when Leo nudged my side with his elbow.

Too late, because Smelly Toes was already standing in front of me, reaching out her hand. "Since when are phones allowed in the classroom, Clara?" she asked.

I wanted to reply, "Since you made my best friend move away", but I didn't dare. Instead I placed my phone in her hand and stared at my worksheet.

"You can pick it up from the office after school," said Smelly Toes, as she headed to the front of the class.

Of course, Vivi and Sarah giggled at my stupidity, and I had the feeling that this second day of school without my best friend was turning out to be even worse than the first one.

I glanced at Leo, who shrugged sympathetically, and thought of Mr King's question: what was so bad about my new desk mate? After all, this was the second time this morning he had been kind.

Smelly Toes was explaining which word belonged in which gap on the worksheet, but I couldn't concentrate at all. I thought of Lottie and how she was sitting all alone in her classroom with no one to talk to. It was bad enough to go somewhere new and not know anyone, but if the other kids weren't even interested in talking to you...I looked back at Leo. I hadn't been very nice to him, even though there was really no reason for it. Now he was rummaging in his backpack, and before I knew it, he was passing me his phone.

"So you can reply," he whispered, pretending to be listening to the teacher.

I gratefully accepted his phone.

Unfortunately, Leo's phone was a different model to mine, so even after pressing various buttons, I couldn't find the messaging menu. Because I didn't want to attract Smelly Toes's attention again, I passed the phone back to him. Leo looked at it, and I looked at Leo – it was actually inevitable that Smelly Toes would notice something suspicious. Anyway, there she was, standing in front of our desk again, her hand outstretched. *Oh no*, I thought. I could tell what was going to happen next.

"Funny," she said. "I've been here before. Leo, the same applies to you as to Clara. You can pick up your phone from the office after school. And before anyone else is tempted: Clara and Leo will have detention for an hour at the end of the day. If you want to join them, all you have to do is get your phone out."

I gulped. Taking our phones off us was one thing... but detention? Normally Nino and Darius were the only ones who ever got detention, when they'd really caused trouble. That was completely different to a tiny peek at a phone, surely? My ears went bright red and I stared at the tabletop. Ugh, this awful smelly woman.

Before she could threaten us with anything else, the bell rang for break.

I turned to Leo immediately. "I'm really sorry you got detention too," I blurted.

"No worries," he answered. "After all, if there are two of us detention is only half as boring."

Then he took a big bite of his Nutella sandwich and disappeared into the fray.

* * *

When I went to the bookshop after school, it seemed like they were all waiting for me.

"Clara!" miaowed Gustaf reproachfully. "Where have you been my dear girl? It's Tuesday and you always bring me..."

Oh no, I had forgotten Gustaf's cinnamon swirl! On Tuesdays, and only on Tuesdays, there were cinnamon swirls at the bakery next to our school. These were Gustaf's favourite thing in the world, so I always bought him one on my way home from school.

I sat down beside his armchair. "Gustaf, I'm so sorry! I had to stay behind for detention today and I completely forgot. Shall I go back?"

"No need," grumbled the cat, "I see your good intention. But tell me why you got detention."

"I'm also intrigued to hear why," interrupted Mr King. "Does this have anything to do with your new teacher by any chance?"

While I was telling them what had happened, Mrs Owl came in from the office, humming and waving a book in the air. "Look at this! A lovely new book on Swedish baking. It just came in today!"

"What?" Gustaf shouted, suddenly no longer interested in my story. He leaped up on to the table with the new releases and stood with his front legs poised on a stack of comics to get a better look at the new book.

"Oh heaven's above; I think I'm in love!" he shouted. "*Kladdkaka, chokladbollar* and *prinsesstårta.*"

It was all Greek to me. Well, Swedish.

Gustaf had a penchant for Sweden and always claimed that he was named after the Swedish king Carl Gustaf. From time to time – mostly when he couldn't think of a rhyme – he cited Swedish proverbs, but you could never tell if they already existed or if he had just invented them. And there was one other phrase he could say in Swedish: "*Jag äter gärna kanelbullar*", which meant "I love cinnamon swirls".

"Perhaps we could try some baking here in the shop," mused Mrs Owl, which made Gustaf jump in the air with joy. "In any case, it's time we had a little party so our customers remember us."

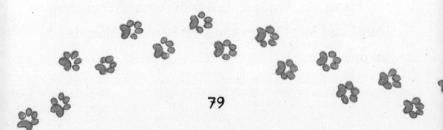

The second she spoke, a craft book, a book about French wines and a psychology self-help book all flung themselves off the shelves. Mrs Owl laughed and her eyes sparkled, like they did whenever an idea formed in her mind. There was nothing she loved more than to think up a crazy plan for something that would make other people happy. Sometimes she rustled something up in such a short space of time that I wondered if she had magical abilities or if her day contained more than twenty-four hours. Once she invited a whole host of literary lookalikes, and the shop was full of the doppelgängers of long-dead authors. They all read extracts from their books and chatted with the guests. And they looked so deceptively real, I could have sworn that they weren't just lookalikes but were the authors themselves: Roald Dahl with his baggy cardigan or Erich Kästner with his bushy eyebrows. That was impossible, of course. But somehow Mrs Owl managed it all so effortlessly and the customers loved it.

"Hmm, yes, I'm sure we'll come up with something nice," said Mrs Owl, putting the Swedish baking book to one side.

"What about a mirror that reads fairy tales to children?" asked Mr King.

"Tales of fur that would make our friends purr?" said Gustaf.

"A romantic evening where a mirror reads amorous love stories?" suggested Mr King.

"An evening of culinary delight with feline food stories to excite?" added Gustaf.

"A spine-tingling crime night," said Mr King, "where a mirror reads from the latest gripping thrillers?"

"A finger-licking feast: a taste of the East?" suggested Gustaf. "Try a bit of this and that. And don't forget to feed the cat?"

We thought up some more nonsensical ideas and got sillier and sillier. I hadn't laughed so much since Lottie moved away, and that felt really good.

I didn't know how much time had passed, but eventually the bell above the shop door rang, and Gustaf shouted, "So late in the day...A customer – hooray!"

Mrs Owl jumped up from her chair and quickly wiped away her tears of laughter, as I scrambled up to the children's books corner to admire the colourful rows of books.

Mr King immediately began his clairvoyant spiel. "Aha, this one's head over heels in love. She gets palpitations at just the thought of her sweetheart. But she's not after a book for him, but for someone she's worried about. She's already got a couple of wrinkles from worrying. She wants to cheer this person up."

I craned my neck to see what a head-over-heels-in-love customer looked like, but it would have been better if I hadn't. Because there, in the middle of the shop, stood...Smelly Toes. I tried to hide behind a cardboard tree house that Mrs Owl had set up as a decoration, but Smelly Toes had already spotted me.

"Hello, Clara," she said gently. "How nice to see you here! It was a bit of a long day for you today." She winked at me as if she'd cracked a joke.

"Oh no," said Mr King, who suddenly realised who this customer was.

She was wearing the same pinafore dress as this morning and her hair was up in a ponytail. She ran her fingers over the books as she walked around looking at the shop. "It's lovely in here," she said.

Mrs Owl had been lurking in the background, either because she was waiting for more information from Mr

King or because she wanted to sense if the customer already knew what she wanted.

"Keep her away from Clara!" the mirror ordered. "She's already in a sweat, she's so upset."

I noticed Gustaf make the most of the shop door being open to scarper outside. If only I could run out after him!

Mrs Owl stepped energetically into Smelly Toes's path. "How can I help you?" she asked, and then went on to answer her own question. "I could recommend a good book." She tried to guide Smelly Toes in the direction of the chick lit. However, she wasn't distracted and headed for the small staircase that led up to the children's mezzanine, thereby blocking my only escape route.

"Thanks," she said. "I do need a book, but in this case Clara is the expert who can help me."

I stared transfixed at the book in my hand, pretending to be studying the title intently. But what *really* interested me was why Smelly Toes thought *I* would be able to help her choose a book.

"Oh, yes?" asked Mrs Owl. "Why's that then?"

"You're going to have to go through with this now,

Clara," said Mr King reassuringly. "But you can do it. She's harmless really – believe me, I can tell."

Perhaps Smelly Toes could somehow hide her evil side so the mirror couldn't see it.

"Yes, I'm looking for a nice book for the daughter of my..." she hesitated for a moment, "of my friend."

I suddenly felt really sick.

"You must know Lottie's taste in books, right? I'd like to send her a little package to help her settle into her new home. What do you think she would like?"

I pressed my lips together to stop anything mean from accidentally bursting out of my mouth. How could she be so underhand? It was her fault Lottie had to move from her old home, and now she wanted to send a welcome package to her new one? Did she think that would make everything better?

"Stay calm, Clara," urged Mr King. "This situation is very uncomfortable for her too. She's at least as upset as you are."

"But I haven't taken anybody's best friend away!" I said loudly, staring defiantly at Smelly Toes.

It didn't seem to trouble her that this wasn't an answer to her question.

"Clara, I know Lottie is your best friend and you're probably mad at me for her moving away."

She took a step on to the small staircase and I instinctively backed away.

"I understand that. I really do. I also wish there had been another solution. But it's the way it is, and we should try to make the best of it."

I felt tears in my eyes. Smelly Toes had no idea! No idea how stupid you feel without a best friend...and how lonely.

Mrs Owl pushed past Ms Rose and came upstairs to put her arm around me. And then I started crying. I missed Lottie so much and didn't want to have this Smelly Toes as a teacher or Leo as a desk mate or...

"Maybe you'd better come back another time," said Mrs Owl, and Smelly Toes nodded.

"Yes, that's probably best." She swallowed hard. "I'm really sorry."

"Can you see that?" asked Mr King. "She's got tears in her eyes as well! She's really serious."

Smelly Toes hung her head and walked slowly towards the door.

"Hell's bells, what's going on? I've only been five

minutes gone!" shouted Gustaf, who had sprung back into the shop. "Clara, there's no need to cry, Gustaf is here and cheer you up he'll try."

My sobs mingled with a small laugh.

"Come on," said Mr King. "Tell her at least one thing that would make Lottie happy. Nobody should leave our shop feeling sad."

Best of all, Lottie liked adventure stories or fantasy worlds with mighty wizards.

"Snakes," I said in a teary voice that didn't sound like mine.

Smelly Toes turned to face me. "What was that?"

"Snakes. Lottie is really interested in snakes."

A small smile crossed my teacher's face. "Thank you," she said.

I almost felt sorry for her. Because if there was one thing Lottie hated, it was snakes.

6

SAVING PODGE

Without the afternoon cheer-up sessions with Mrs Owl, Gustaf and Mr King, I'm not sure how I would have survived the first week back at school. And I certainly wouldn't have managed without my Lottie and Clara friendship book, my phone and Finn's computer (which he sometimes graciously let me use).

Lottie told me on the phone about her new school and the stupid girl she had to sit next to, and I told her about our old school and about the not-so-stupid boy I had to sit next to. By now I'd realised that Leo was actually pretty cool, but of course no matter how nice he was, he wasn't Lottie.

So the first week of school was over and finally it was the weekend. On the one hand, I was relieved, because I could have a break from Vivi and Sarah's idiotic chatter, and I could hang out at the bookshop all day on Saturday. On the other hand, I always spent most of the weekends with Lottie – we would make waffles, get dressed up or set up a jumble sale on the street. One of our favourite ways to spend the weekend was taking Podge out for a walk. But it was never just going for a walk. We would always imagine we were somewhere else, like in Paris or in an underground city or in some kind of lush tropical paradise. We would really get into character and put on the appropriate silly accents, so on our walk through Paris, Lottie would say, "Ah, *mon dieu*, isn't it beautiful how the Eiffel Tower glints in the sun?" And I would say, "*Oui*, it's *magnifique*! Shall we get a baguette for *le dîner* on the way home?"

Perhaps I could spend the weekend with Lottie, in my thoughts at least, if I took Podge out for a walk and daydreamed about being somewhere else.

So, early that Saturday morning, I called out, "I'll go and get some bread rolls!" That was a tradition for our family breakfast together.

I had no idea if anyone had heard me – Dad had already barricaded himself in his darkroom, Mum was blow-drying her hair in the bathroom and I hadn't seen the others yet.

"Come on, Podge," I called.

The chubby black mongrel with floppy ears slowly emerged from his little basket under the coat rack. He waddled over to me so slowly, he looked like he might fall back asleep at any moment. I waved his leash at him in the hope he would be excited by the prospect of some exercise, but I knew he probably would have preferred a nice liverwurst sandwich. So I clipped on his leash against his will and dragged him out of the front door.

This time I imagined I had landed in an eerie vampire city. It was dark, and I pictured Lottie and me holding hands as we gingerly tiptoed down a deserted lane dimly lit by old-fashioned street lamps.

The street lamps were a key theme of our real walk, because unfortunately Podge wanted to stop and sniff each one extensively, which didn't really fit with my vampire city story. At this rate I doubted whether we'd even make it to the bakery before they sold out of bread. I considered tying Podge up and hurrying to pick up the rolls on my own, but I couldn't do that to the poor little guy. So I waited patiently until he had given everything a thorough sniff, and meanwhile to help pass the time I tried imagining I was in London and, when that didn't work, I pictured Pippi Longstocking's house, but basically I couldn't concentrate at all. Somehow Lottie and I would have to catch up with each other in real life – perhaps we would be able to Skype later or maybe I could persuade Mum and Dad to let me go and visit her soon.

When we finally got to the bakery, I tied Podge to a park bench a few metres away and went into the shop. I'd done this loads of times before, and yet this faithful companion of a dog looked up at me with such sad eyes, as if I were saying goodbye forever.

There was an enormous queue and I had to wait for what seemed like an eternity. I tried to keep an eye on Podge through the window, but the cars parked outside blocked my view. When it was finally my turn, I rattled out my order at top speed then dashed out with the bag of bread under my arm without even waiting for my change.

Straight away I saw that Podge was no longer tied to the bench where I'd left him. Oh no. Oh no. Oh no!

I started running, faster and faster, calling out, "Podge! Where are you? Podgeeeee, I'm here!"

Panicked, I spun round, looking around, because he couldn't have gone far. My heart was pounding wildly. "Podge? Podge? Where are you?!"

Then I heard a heartbreaking whimper and at the same time a spiteful cackle. On the grass next to the youth centre I spotted three older boys who I recognised from Finn's school. They were standing in a circle and were throwing and catching something. I couldn't see what it was, but it had to be something that Podge really wanted, because he was leaping between their feet and whining like crazy.

"Well, you little fatty? You need to work out a bit, mate!" one of the boys teased him, throwing something floppy to his friend.

It was a salami sausage! I had no idea where they'd got it from, but I did know that Podge would do anything for a sausage.

"Come on then! Come and get it, fatso!" shouted one of the other boys.

I could hardly bear to watch poor Podge desperately trying to catch it. I ran towards the boys on the grass.

"Hey, stop that!" I shouted as I approached them.

"What do you want, brat?" one of them asked with a menacing grin.

"I want my dog back!" I shouted angrily.

"That's not a dog! That's a bowling ball on four legs!" The boys all laughed. "Besides, we're just having a laugh. You can have your Podgeball back in a minute."

"Podge, come here!" I ordered, trying to attract his attention.

But the dog wasn't interested in me at all, only in the sausage.

"Please stop it," I said, looking at the boys.

"No way!"

"Podge," I called desperately, feeling the tears well up in my eyes. These guys were much taller and stronger than me. What if they just took Podge with them?

"What's going on?" I heard a familiar voice behind me. "Leave the dog alone and get lost!"

I turned around. "Leo!" I felt like giving him a hug I was so pleased to see him.

"Who are you?" growled the leader of the gang. "Come to save your little friend?"

I blushed – embarrassed, but also angry. Emboldened by Leo's presence, I strode towards Podge, utterly fearless. Even though I was at least two heads shorter than them, I walked straight into the middle of their circle and grabbed at the sausage with one hand as it whooshed through the air. Then I bit into it with relish, before passing it over to Leo. The boys just stared at me in confusion.

"Hey, spoilsport!" one shouted, while the other two just gave up and strutted off across the park.

Podge was baffled and rather unimpressed that the sausage had stopped flying about, but when he realised that Leo had it, he leaped up against his leg and whimpered.

"Come on then. Come back to Clara," Leo called, luring Podge behind him with the sausage as bait.

When they were at my side, Leo held the sausage in front of Podge's nose, and – snap! – it was gone.

"Thanks," I said, smiling at Leo. "That was pretty cool of you to show up."

"You should play handball," Leo said with a grin. "Although you don't normally have to snatch sausages away from your opponent – usually it's a ball."

"Oh, great," I said. "Maybe I should try it in case anyone tries teasing Podge like that again."

"The girls' team trains on Thursdays at four," Leo said, walking to his bike, which he had leaned against a tree. "Think about it." He got on his bike and pedalled off. "See you on Monday!" he shouted, and then he was gone.

When I got home, my family was already waiting. As soon as I put the bread rolls on the table, they threw themselves at them as if they hadn't eaten for weeks.

"Why were you out so long?" asked Mum, but I didn't feel like telling her the real reason.

"It was really busy," I said, and it wasn't exactly a lie. I sat down at the table.

Mum shrugged and then went back to leafing through a catalogue.

Dad was studying the newspaper and absent-mindedly dipping his croissant into Jacob's apple juice.

"Hey, look, Clara – your bookshop's in the paper," he said. "Oh, what a great idea!" He slid the page over and tapped his finger on a small advert on the classifieds page.

> We LOVE our customers! That's why we're offering you a free book today. All you need to do is dress up as your favourite character from a book and come to our shop between eleven and twelve o'clock on Saturday. We look forward to seeing your costumes!
>
> ~ Your favourite bookshop

I smiled. Yes, that sounded like Mrs Owl! The idea must have come to her last night, because she didn't mention a word about it while I was in the shop.

"What is it?" asked Grandma, nosily peeking over my shoulder. No one in our family was nosier than Grandma. She never missed a thing and stuck her nose into everything, although she tended to forget half of it straight away. Grandma clapped her hands with excitement. "Oh, dear Mrs Owl! Another brilliant idea! I'm there!"

"Me too!" declared Dad.

The fact that our family was noisy probably didn't set us apart from other families, but the fact that we all loved dressing up was rather unique. Everyone except Mum, that is. And at the moment Finn too, because he was going through puberty. But if it was up to Dad and Grandma, every family party would be a themed dressing-up party.

"I'll go and get changed," said Dad. He leaped up from the table so fast my eyes could hardly follow him, almost knocking over his coffee cup, and hurried off down the hall.

Mum watched him, shaking her head. "So this is what a lazy Saturday morning breakfast looks like, is it?" she muttered, returning to her catalogue.

"What are you going to dress up as?" I asked Grandma, who was secretly tossing Podge a piece of her salami roll.

"Dressing up? I want to dress up too!" cried Jacob, waving his chocolate-smeared hands wildly in the air. "I'm a pirate!"

Grandma wiped her mouth with a napkin. "And I'm going to be Sister...Sister Thingamajig!"

"You mean Sister Ingeborg?"

"That's what I said," said Grandma.

Sister Ingeborg was the nurse in the series Grandma was always reading.

Again I thought of Lottie. If she was living here, I would have called her immediately. We would have made fantastic costumes together. Perhaps we would have gone as the vampire sisters. Now I had to decide on my own who I wanted to be, and that wasn't easy at all because I had lots of favourite characters.

But at least my Saturday was saved, even without Lottie. Because going to one of Mrs Owl's parties with Dad in disguise, Grandma in a nurse's uniform and Jacob as a pirate certainly sounded like it was going to be a good laugh.

"So, everyone who wants to dress up, off you go," said Mum as she began to clear up the dishes. "Everyone else is helping me."

I had to giggle when I saw Finn's face. I ran up to my room, bumping into Dad in the hall. He was wearing the same jeans as before and had just put on a different T-shirt. He had also hung his camera around his neck.

"I thought you were going to dress up," I said.

"I have," he replied.

"As who?" I asked.

"I'm going as Friedrich Jacobsen."

Friedrich Jacobsen was going as himself.

"You can't," I said. "It said you have to dress up as your favourite character from a book. And you're not —"

"Not yet!" said Dad with a big grin. "But soon I will be! I've been working on my biography for some time now." He pushed past me and sauntered back into the kitchen, whistling to himself.

I stood in front of the bookshelf in my room which could almost compete with the children's books corner in Mrs Owl's shop – maybe not in terms of the number of books but the variety. And that was thanks to Mrs Owl. She was always giving me books that I would never have chosen for myself. Like the one with the cat in space, for example.

I ran my index finger along the shelf until one caught my fancy. And then I knew who I was going to dress up as: if I didn't have my vampire sister, then I would go as Velda the vampire princess.

7

VELDA THE VAMPIRE PRINCESS

It was half an eternity before we were all dressed up and ready to go. My costume was by far the most elaborate, and now I looked almost exactly like Velda on the front cover of the book. Mum let me wear one of her old black dresses – first she cut a strip off at the bottom to make it shorter and to look more ragged. She also quickly sewed on a few purple and pink tulle strips and helped me make a crown out of wire and aluminium foil.

We must have looked pretty funny when we stepped out of the house on to the street – a vampire princess, a pirate, a nurse and a photographer. If only Lottie had been there too! But anyway, it felt good to at least have some of my family as company – it was a rare occasion that we all went together to Mrs Owl's

Bookshop. It was a pity that Mum and Finn didn't come too.

Although it usually took me only three minutes to get there, it took about ten times as long this time. Every time we walked two steps, Dad held up his hand like a traffic cop, shouting, "Stand still please!" Then he'd drop to his knees or stand on tiptoe or somehow contort his body in some strange way to take a picture of us. In the beginning we all played along and stood in sensible poses, but after a few photos we started pulling silly faces and twisted into bizarre poses, which looked especially funny with Grandma.

"These pics are going to be legendary," shouted Dad enthusiastically, running backwards with the camera in front of his face. It wasn't until he bumped his backside against an electrical junction box that he finally put down his camera with an "Ooh, that hurt!" and we were able to walk the last few metres without interruption.

We were all in high spirits when we arrived at the bookshop and I jumped in the air with joy when I saw how busy it was. People were pouring into the shop, which was about to burst at the seams. Mr King wouldn't be able to keep up with his analysis of everyone who came in; I imagined he was already dizzy from all the people passing by. I spotted a Snow White, two trolls, some Jedi knights, a sailor and someone else who also looked exactly like Velda the vampire princess. A few people had really impressive costumes, while some looked as if they'd come as themselves, like Dad. There were probably a lot of new autobiographies coming out next year.

"Clara!" Gustaf shouted, excitedly running to meet us. I was surprised to see he hadn't dressed up – I'd expected King Gustaf or at least a character from a Swedish children's book. "It's really great you're here! Look at this mayhem – oh dear!"

I had to get rid of the others so that I could answer him. "Why don't you go in and get your books?" I suggested.

Grandma launched herself into the fray, holding Jacob by the hand. Dad had already disappeared and was eagerly taking pictures of the guests.

"What a fantastic idea," I said when everyone was out of earshot. "I've never seen the shop so busy! And it looks like everyone's having a great time!"

"Now they are," said Gustaf, who seemed jumpy as he paced back and forth. "But, Clara, things won't stay that way, when they learn there's nought to give away!"

"What?" I asked. "How can that be? It said so in the paper."

"It wasn't Mrs Owl who placed the ad! It must have been someone really bad. Mrs Owl can't give so many books away – she would be bankrupt in a day."

Goodness me, that was true! Why hadn't that occurred to me? This wasn't the great idea that it had seemed after all.

I stood on tiptoe to get a better look at the shop. "So what now?"

"I don't know, I don't know," moaned Gustaf. "I only hope it won't end in woe!"

Gustaf tended to see everything very negatively. He's a glass-half-empty kind of cat.

"Come on, let's go in," I said. "Mrs Owl is sure to think of something."

I picked up Gustaf, so that no one would step on his paws, and edged my way slowly through the crowd.

"Welcome, welcome!" I heard Mrs Owl call. "How

wonderful that you've all found your way to my book-shop." Her voice was as cheerful as ever.

She waved to me and I fought my way over with Gustaf.

Mrs Owl's plait was a bit dishevelled, but she was beaming and stood there in her green dress like a queen. "What a surprise!" she said softly. "But, as you know, there's nothing I love more than surprises!"

"But...but...all these people who came rushing!" mi-aowed Gustaf. "They'll be furious when they get nothing!"

"My dear Gustaf," said Mrs Owl, patting the cat affectionately on the head, "we'll just have to be crea-tive. Stretch those little feline brain cells! If we put our heads together we'll think of something."

I looked around and watched the people crowding in front of the shelves, leafing through books or gath-ering in groups to be photographed by Dad. Everyone really was in a good mood. Everyone but Gustaf and Mr King.

"Fingers off!" shouted Mr King. Three girls had ap-peared in front of him and one was gently stroking his golden frame. "I can't bear it," he wailed. "I'm covered with greasy fingerprints from top to bottom. A little boy even pressed his nose against me earlier. Ugh! You do not want to know what I saw there!"

Mrs Owl began to laugh out loud, squealing and wheezing, and I couldn't help but laugh too. At first people looked at us questioningly, but somehow our laughter seemed to be so contagious that soon two older ladies were chuckling too, and the three girls in front of the mirror, and then it seemed to pass around the shop like a chain reaction, until the whole bookshop was laughing. I had never seen anything like it. Some people had tears in their eyes and were slapping their thighs, and I could even see people outside on the street giggling.

There was just one person who didn't even smile. One man who looked as gloomy as seven days of rain. Mr Schwartz stood in the middle of the shop. I suddenly realised whose idea the ad must have been. But why would he do such a thing? Whatever he had intended, his plan seemed to have backfired.

Chuckling, I tapped on Mrs Owl's shoulder to point him out. As he turned to leave, shaking his head with contempt, she shouted a cheerful "*Arrivederci!*" after him.

You need to be smart if you want to pick a fight with Mrs Owl.

"Bye-bye, Mr Schwartz Farts!" shouted Gustaf, who had obviously cheered up with all the laughing.

But among all the chuckles, snorts and giggles, I also started to hear the question that I had been afraid of all this time.

"So, when are we going to get our books?" one woman asked.

Other people stopped laughing and looked at us expectantly.

Mrs Owl quickly clambered up on to the counter. She wiped the last tears of laughter from her cheek and cleared her throat. "First of all, let me say how delighted I am that you've all found your way to us and are having such a lovely time in our bookshop. Your costumes are a sensation! It's simply wonderful to see so many different fictional characters in the shop!"

"Well, if that isn't worth a round of applause!" Dad shouted and started to clap.

A few people joined in, while the others carried on listening quietly.

"However, we've had to change the plan ever so slightly. Of course, everyone may take a book, as promised in the ad, but..."

What on earth was she going to say next?

"I'd like to draw attention to our piggy bank here –" it was a mystery to me where that had come from so quickly, but suddenly there was a huge, pink porcelain pig on the counter "– and ask you to pop something in, as much as you think the book deserves. Agreed?"

"Brilliant!" cried Mr King enthusiastically. "An ingenious idea, Mrs Owl!"

"Profit, you say? You'd give it to who?" Gustaf's ears perked up. "I'm sure I could think of a bun or two!"

"We'll worry about that later," whispered Mrs Owl. "The most important thing now is that people leave the shop satisfied."

There was an approving murmur throughout the crowd. No one seemed upset or annoyed. People nodded and pulled out their wallets and soon there was a jingle as the first coins fell into the piggy bank.

"Of course, you could always bring the money in afterwards, when you've read the book!" added Mrs Owl. "And if you don't like it, you pay nothing."

She climbed back down from the counter and smoothed her dress out. "And please don't stand on my toes," she said under her breath.

The first guests were edging their way towards the exit, where they were halted by Dad with a "Stop, stop, stop!" He flourished his camera. "Don't go yet! Let's have a group photo for the local paper with *all* the book characters! Shall we all gather in front of the shop window? We don't get an opportunity like this every day!" He winked at Mrs Owl.

"Thank you, Clara," said Mrs Owl.

"Why?" I asked. "I haven't done anything."

She smiled contentedly. "Oh, you have."

I couldn't help laughing. "You're welcome then."

Through the shop window I could see my father lining everyone up for the photo.

"You must certainly be in the photo, my dear," Gustaf said to me. "And to represent the shop, I'll volunteer! You can't, of course, Mr King – you're stuck to the wall on a string."

"Not funny!" said Mr King, offended. "But anyway, I couldn't possibly appear in the newspaper in this state. I'm smothered in horrid greasy marks!"

"I'll clean you up – don't you worry," said Mrs Owl.

So Gustaf and I went to the door, and Dad placed us at the side of the group.

"Hmpf, I should be sitting in the middle of you all," grumbled Gustaf, "as representative of the shop and mascot of its soul."

"Nonsense," I reassured him. "You'd get lost in the photo down there. This position shows you off perfectly."

The cat sat up straight and stretched his neck to show his best side. "Is my coat nice and sleek?" he asked. "Any stray hairs need a tweak?"

"You look perfect," I said, and I looked down the row of people. And that's when I spotted her.

The other Velda. She was about the same height as me and must have been about my age. Unlike me, she was wearing a wig, which made her look even more like the real Velda.

Suddenly, I had a funny fidgety feeling in my stomach. If Velda was her favourite novel, then she had good taste in books. It was the same with Lottie and me, so it seemed like a sound basis for a friendship. If your best friend lent you a book or gave you one, you could count on it being good. Of course, I would never find a replacement for Lottie, and I didn't want to either, but maybe it wouldn't hurt to know another nice girl who I could meet up with every now and then, and maybe we could swap books?

"On the count of three, smile!" shouted Dad, as by now everyone had streamed out of the shop and was lined up ready for the photo. He took a few snaps and then said, "Thank you, ladies and gentlemen. All done. Keep your eyes peeled for the picture in the newspaper!"

The group gradually broke up and I made my way towards the other Velda. Maybe today was my lucky day, even if it had had a rather strange start.

I kept a firm eye on her glittery silver crown, but then I lost sight of it when a James Bond stepped between us. By the time I'd pushed past him and his Martini glass, Velda had disappeared.

"Velda?" I called, looking around.

I spotted Jacob, who was fencing with a bandit, and Grandma, who was engrossed in an animated conversation with a Dr Bernhardt from the same series she loves, but the vampire princess had vanished into thin air. Just like she did in the book – that girl had clearly taken her costume very seriously. A feeling of disappointment settled deep inside.

"Don't hang your head so low," said Gustaf, trying to cheer me up, "or like a giraffe your neck will grow."

I didn't feel like laughing, but Gustaf wasn't giving up.

"Speaking of which, why do giraffes have such long necks?"

I shook my head.

"Because their heads are so high up!" he laughed his screeching cat-laugh just as he always did when he found one of his own jokes particularly funny.

I crouched down next to him. "You're the best cat in the world," I said, giving him a tickle behind the ears.

Just the fact that he had tried to cheer me up was reason enough to love him. "Let's go back in and help Mrs Owl clean up."

The day had been so eventful that I couldn't possibly write it all down in my friendship book. When I got home, I'd already thought of how I could bribe Finn to let me use his computer. But it turned out I didn't need to – he wasn't there.

"Where's Finn?" I asked Grandma, who was sitting in the armchair in her room watching TV.

"Shhh, darling, I'm watching my show," she grumbled, her eyes fixed on the screen. "All I'm saying is that when he left the house, there was such a waft of aftershave that it smelled like he was trying to impress an entire girls' boarding school."

I left Grandma's room and held my nose in the air. It really did smell of Dad's aftershave. Did Finn seriously have a date with a girl? I could hardly believe it. But I'd think about that later, because right now I had to talk to Lottie.

Luckily she was online so I could call her right away over Skype.

"You won't believe all the crazy things that happened today," I gushed.

I told her about the newspaper ad, how we had dressed up and about Mrs Owl's reaction to Mr Schwartz's nasty joke. "It was so cool when Mrs Owl said people could all take a book for free. You should have seen their faces!"

I talked and talked, not even noticing that Lottie's mouth was drooping lower and lower.

"You're having so much fun without me," said Lottie when she finally had a chance to speak.

"That's not true," I reassured her. Given everything I'd just said, it wasn't very convincing though. "It would have been a hundred times more fun with you, honestly. I thought of you the whole time."

"Doesn't sound like it," said Lottie. She quickly wiped her face with her hand. Was that a tear? "If you're even interested," Lottie said, "things are really rubbish here. I miss my dad and I haven't made a new friend yet."

That felt like a stab in my stomach. "And you don't miss me?" I asked stupidly.

"No, of course I don't miss my best friend," she

snapped. Somehow our conversation was heading in the wrong direction.

"Lottie," I said, "this is all so dumb. We just need to see each other soon!"

"What's the point?" she asked. "It would just make me feel worse."

I didn't know what to say.

"Well, bye then," Lottie said. "Have fun with all the amazing things you're doing." And then she hung up.

I felt even worse than the day I'd said goodbye to my best friend.

8

MRS OWL IS IN TROUBLE

The next week was rainy and grey, and so was my mood. I heard Mrs Owl's voice in my head telling me today was no day to be down in the dumps, but it didn't seem to help. I couldn't get my conversation with Lottie out of my head and it made me feel rotten. We had never quarrelled before or even been mean to each other. Although she had texted me later to say she was sorry and I had also apologised and reassured her about how much I missed her, I still had this stupid, horrible feeling. I was so worried that being apart would ruin our friendship. We needed to do something! If only I had Mrs Owl's talent for hitting on the perfect solution, like on Saturday, when Mr Schwartz had pulled a mean trick on her and she had cleverly turned it into a roaring success.

And yet...it turned out it wasn't such a roaring success after all, because when I went back to the shop that evening, Mrs Owl was really down. People had put money into the piggy bank, but nowhere near enough to cover the cost of the books. It had left a gaping hole in the accounts. Mrs Owl hoped that more customers would come in over the next few days to pay for their books. "Otherwise there'll be a serious problem," she said. I didn't want to even imagine what that meant.

On Thursday I trudged through the drizzle across the school playground to the sports hall, where we had PE. The only good thing about PE was that it wasn't taught by Smelly Toes, but by a nice trainee teacher. Otherwise, it was my least favourite subject. When Lottie was here, it wasn't quite so bad, because my best friend was a real sports star. Whenever we had to do something in pairs, she would be my partner, and whenever it came to choosing teams, she would pick me for hers. So I always felt I could sort of hide in her shadow.

When I changed clothes and entered the sports hall, a queasy feeling spread through my stomach. Mr Borchers had got the handballs out and the class was already bouncing them around or throwing them at each other. I was a bit hopeless at throwing and catching, so I went and sat down on a bench.

"Please get into pairs and face each other!" shouted Mr Borchers.

I hoped we were an odd number so I might be left over and could perhaps stay sitting on the bench. Everyone paired up into the usual couples (Vivi and Sarah, Nora and Lea, Nino and Darius...) and it quickly became clear someone would be left without a partner.

"Vivi and Sarah, will you go in a three with Clara and keep swapping round?" said Mr Borchers, blowing his whistle.

Hmm, I'd been too quick to celebrate. I was watching the two of them throw the ball back and forth when the door opened.

"Ah, perfect!" called Mr Borchers. "Leo! Clara hasn't got a partner yet. Will you two come over here?"

Reluctantly, I got up from the bench and stood on the black line. Hadn't Leo told me that he played handball? This was going to be so embarrassing.

"Are you ready?" Leo asked, and I nodded.

He picked up the ball and threw it in my direction.

Not too strong and not too weak, but just right so that I could catch it. *First time lucky*, I thought, and threw the ball back. It only went as far as the midline, but Leo sprinted to the ball and managed to catch it.

"Not bad," he said. "Just a bit of training and you'll also be able to catch a sausage mid-air when you're out with Podge."

I had to laugh and then I also caught the next ball that Leo threw me.

"Now back to me with a bit more oomph, OK?" he called.

I summoned up all my strength, and the ball flew in a high arc towards Leo, who looked up and held his arms outstretched. My throw went even further than expected, so Leo took a few steps back with his arms out – not seeing Darius and Nino's ball rolling on the floor behind him.

"Careful!" I shouted, but Leo stepped on it and went straight over.

"Ow!" he shouted, his face contorted with pain. "My ankle!"

Mr Borchers came running over and pulled Leo's shoe off. "Can you move it?"

"Yes," Leo said.

"It'll need a cold press," Mr Borchers said. "Clara, run into the teachers' changing room and get a gel pack from the fridge!"

Mr Borchers had probably never seen me run so fast. In no time at all, I was back with the cold gel pack.

"Thanks," said Leo, sitting on the bench with his leg extended.

"I'm so sorry!" I said, feeling really upset. I'd always been rubbish at sport but never so bad that I'd hurt someone.

Leo pressed the cooling pad against his ankle. "Oh, it's not that bad. And it wasn't your fault that I tripped."

"If I hadn't done such a rubbish throw..."

"Nonsense, stop it! I've seen much worse throws at handball practice!" He grinned. "Next time we train, let's stick to a packet of sausages in the park. Deal?" Leo held out his hand to me.

"Deal," I said and shook his hand. Like a true sportsman.

But even though he'd been really kind about it, I could hardly concentrate for the rest of the day at school. I felt so guilty about Leo and desperately hoped his handball career wasn't ruined.

When Smelly Toes entered the classroom for the fourth lesson, I felt the anger boil up inside me. If Lottie were still here, PE would have been completely different. Leo wouldn't be limping, I wouldn't be feeling terrible and everyone would be perfectly happy. Of course, the spat between me and Lottie wouldn't have happened either. Did Smelly Toes have any idea how much damage she had caused? I decided it was time to tell her. Sometimes you just have to vent your anger, Mrs Owl once said, so you can think straight again.

So I went up to her after the lesson and asked if I could have one of those glittery notebooks after all.

"Of course!" said Smelly Toes exuberantly. "I think I've still got two left." She rummaged around in her big bag and I wondered what else she carried around with her besides the glittery books. Flower seeds or cutlery or a flashlight or teabags...? "Here they are!" she said, brushing some biscuit crumbs from the cover. "Which one would you like?"

"Red," I said, almost tearing it out of her hand.

Then, although it was break time, I went and sat with my notebook and started writing down everything that was going round my head. It was a lot. So much that I didn't even notice when the break ended and everyone stormed back into class.

"Were you sitting here the whole time?" asked Leo, dropping into his chair.

He glanced out of the corner of his eye at what I was writing, but I quickly put my arm over it.

"Don't worry, I'm not in the slightest bit interested in girly secrets." He grinned. "Except my sister's."

I had to grin too. "I can think of a brother like that."

He searched his pocket for something. "Then we understand each other," he said, satisfied. "Chocolate?"

"I owe *you* some chocolate," I said. "A giant slab to say sorry."

"Oh, I wouldn't say no." Leo laughed. "Not because you need to say sorry. Just because I'm nuts about chocolate!"

I had an idea. Thanks to Mrs Owl, I knew where you could get the best chocolate treats. I would pay a visit to Chocolate Heaven and get Leo a present to make up for my handball blunder.

By the time I'd finished writing, I had filled three pages and felt a huge relief. I hadn't left anything out, and if Smelly Toes collected in our notebooks, she might finally realise what she'd done. And maybe she would see that it would be better to split up with Lottie's dad so that Lottie's mum and my best friend could come back home where they belonged.

After school, as always, I went to the bookshop. I thought again of all the guests in fancy dress who had come at the weekend, and of the chaos that had ensued. And the girl who had dressed up as Velda and sadly hadn't become my new friend. Maybe she would come to the shop again sometime soon. But would I recognise her without her disguise? Maybe Mr King could help me with his clairvoyant skills.

"On this fine day, a customer – hooray! Oh, Clara, it's you," said Gustaf from his chair.

I closed the door behind me and immediately noticed that something was different. My eyes wandered along the shelves – everything looked the same. Then it struck me: there was a strange silence. Normally you could always hear something:

the patter of Gustaf's paws on the wooden floor, the rustle of paper, the creak of the tape dispenser or Mr King talking.

Then Mrs Owl came out of her office, sat down on the steps and rested her head in her hands. I had never seen her like this before.

"Has something happened?" I asked, worried.

"It's half past one and there hasn't been a single customer today," said Mrs Owl quietly. "It's been like this the whole week."

"What?" I exclaimed. Thursdays were usually busy, because people had finished their books and needed something new for the weekend. "But the event on Saturday went really well. And Dad told me that his photo was going to be in the paper today!"

"Sadly not," said Mrs Owl. "But they did print an anonymous letter, in which the sender complained that the newspaper ad was misleading, saying it promised free books but in fact they had to be paid for. And that Mrs Owl's Bookshop was trying to attract customers by deceit." Mrs Owl swallowed. "Besides, the event didn't bring in enough money. Unless a miracle happens, I don't know how I'm going to pay the rent for the shop next month."

I felt completely sick to the stomach. What if no more customers came after the complaint in the newspaper? What if Mrs Owl really couldn't pay her rent any more? And what if she didn't have any money for new books? If Mrs Owl had to close her shop...? That must not be allowed to happen under any circumstances! This shop belonged to our town as much as the church in the marketplace or the town hall!

The yellow butterfly, which hadn't left its cover for a while, fluttered over and sat on Mrs Owl's shoulder to comfort her.

As if the whole situation wasn't bad enough, at that moment the shop door opened and a thunderous voice called out, "Well, isn't this a lovely day?"

"Get out!" shouted Mr King, which of course the intruder couldn't hear.

Mrs Owl got up, smoothed down her green dress and in a friendly voice asked, "Mr Schwartz, what can I do for you today?"

The troublemaker looked around as if he were actually looking for a book. Eventually, however, his gaze settled on Mr King. "I have the feeling," said Mr Schwartz, "that things aren't going so well here at the shop." He sniggered maliciously. "I just wanted to remind you to bring the mirror to me as soon as you wind down the business."

"I assure you that I shan't be winding down my business or bringing you my mirror. Goodbye!" said Mrs Owl calmly but firmly.

A large fantasy novel hurled itself off the shelf next to Mr Schwartz, flew right past the head of the antiques dealer and crashed on to the floor. Mr Schwartz jumped back, startled.

"I'll report you!" he threatened. "For grievous bodily harm!"

Suddenly something happened that I had never seen before. From the cover of the book that had tumbled down, a waft of greenish, shimmering mist rose up, enveloping Mr Schwartz. He coughed and waved his hands, but the cloud around him just grew bigger and denser.

"Wh-what's this?" he stammered. "A-a-are you trying to poison me?"

"Whatever do you mean?" asked Mrs Owl, pretending to be completely unaware. "Is everything all right?"

"This...this fog! Make it disappear!"

"I can't see any fog, Mr Schwartz. Clara, can you see anything?"

"No," I said, holding back a laugh.

"This...this will have consequences!" cried Mr Schwartz, stomping out of the shop in a great huff. The fog immediately shrank back into the book cover, as if nothing had happened.

"Ha ha," laughed Gustaf. "That was amazing! I want more! That's a trick I've not seen before!"

I was just about to agree when I looked at Mrs Owl and saw that the lightning spark was gone from her eyes. It had been there a moment ago when we were teasing Mr Schwartz.

"Hey, today's no day to be down in the dumps," I said, but it didn't sound as convincing coming from me as it did from her.

"At least we had some customers in the shop on Saturday and we could speak to them in person, smooth over what Mr Schwartz had done. But if nobody comes in now..." Mrs Owl didn't finish.

"Maybe they will still print Dad's photo," I suggested. "Or we could hold another event to bring customers in."

Mrs Owl sighed and shook her head. She didn't reply. In all the time I'd known her, I'd never seen her so down. She usually had a witty response to everything, wise advice always on the tip of her tongue.

The telephone rang in the office.

"No time to sigh or moan – someone wants you on the phone," rhymed Gustaf, without his usual gusto. He normally bellowed out his rhymes with great enthusiasm, but today he seemed to be just as dispirited as Mrs Owl.

She disappeared into the office and closed the door behind her.

"Oh, Gustaf, what can we do?" I said, as soon as Mrs Owl was out of earshot. "I can't bear to see her like this!" The sick feeling in my stomach muddied my thoughts. If only Lottie were here! She would think of something to get us out of this mess.

"I'm going to go and find Schwartz Farts, and make him pay for his dark arts," growled Gustaf. Determined, he jumped up and ran to the door. "If I'm not back in

half an hour, call the police!
Or else I may not return in one piece!"

"Gustaf," I said, "Mr Schwartz can't understand you!"

"He'll understand me all right!" he answered fiercely. "When I hiss and splay my claws to fight!" He quickly showed us what he had in mind.

"All right, puss, less of the fuss," ordered Mr King. "We mustn't do anything rash now."

"Oh, you can rhyme too," said Gustaf with a laugh. "All right, puss, less of the fuss! Not bad for a beginner. But do you have any better ideas?"

Mr King seemed to mull it over.

Just like me.

"The most important thing is for Mrs Owl to be happy again," I finally said. "Then she'll be able to think of something."

How we were to achieve that, however, was a mystery. Maybe going to Chocolate Heaven and buying a heap of chocolate cake was the only thing I could do right now.

"I know! A poem will be just the thing – think of the joy that it will bring!" Gustaf shouted, leaping back on to his chair.

"She thinks your poems are terrible," grumbled the mirror.

"You might scowl, but not Mrs Owl!" insisted Gustaf.

"Hey, don't argue!" I interjected. "I've just had an idea." I grinned to myself as a plan took shape in my head.

I listened for a moment to check Mrs Owl was still talking on the phone. I hoped it wasn't someone complaining about the event on Saturday.

"So, what's your idea?" asked Gustaf.

"Well —" I began.

Right at that moment Mrs Owl emerged from the office. She didn't look anything like as depressed as before the phone call.

"That was a very nice gentleman from the paper," she explained. "He wanted to ask about what happened here at the weekend. They've received several complaints, always under a different name, but the reporter suspects there's one and the same person behind them all."

"And I think we have a pretty good idea who that person is!" said Mr King indignantly.

"He says he's got a lovely picture from your father, Clara, and he couldn't square it with all the complaints. He wants to come by tomorrow, to interview us and get a picture for himself. Then he's going to write about us."

I felt a tingle of excitement in my fingertips, because all this fit perfectly with my plan, which I could no longer keep to myself.

"Can he come in the evening by any chance?" I asked.

"We'll be closed," said Mrs Owl, looking at me with a frown. Then the corners of her mouth edged ever so slightly upwards. "But am I right in thinking that you've got something in mind?"

I nodded. And then I told them about my idea.

Mrs Owl listened to me spellbound and, after a while, she smiled with delight.

"And we could call it the Moonlight Book Night," I concluded.

"That's the best idea of the day." Mrs Owl came up to me and hugged me. "You are a treasure!" She kissed me on the cheek while Gustaf snuggled up to me.

Mr King murmured, "Splendid, splendid."

I blushed a little.

And then I thought that here in Mrs Owl's book-shop I had the best friends you could imagine. Not the most ordinary friends perhaps, but ones who stood by each other through thick and thin.

9

THE TALKING BUSH

The next day at school, strangely enough, I no longer had that queasy feeling in my stomach all morning. Instead I felt light and happy. Maybe because yesterday I realised that I had some great friends and wasn't as lonely as I sometimes thought. Sure, a girl my age would be different to a bookseller who was probably older than my mum, a clairvoyant mirror and a rhyming cat who thinks he's of royal Swedish descent, but those three were fabulous friends all the same. And perhaps I just had to be patient about making a new friend. Even if being patient wasn't exactly one of my strengths.

Besides, Lottie was still my best friend, even if everything was a bit strange at the moment. Last night we had another phone chat, and I told her about our plan and asked if she could come. Lottie didn't think her mum would let her. Then we quickly changed the subject. Lottie said she'd received a package from Smelly Toes, which included a totally gross book about snakes, but also some sweets, a CD that she thought wasn't bad and a letter that was actually really nice.

When Smelly Toes walked into the classroom for the third lesson, I thought about the snake book and I couldn't help laughing a little bit. After all, she had made an effort – you had to give her that.

"Good morning, all," she greeted us. "I don't know if you've heard, but on Saturday there was a wonderful event at Mrs Owl's Bookshop."

Vivi put her hand up and in her whiny, high-pitched voice she said, "The books were supposed to be given away but it was all a trick. The owner only wanted to get customers into her shop so they would spend money. And my dad – he's a lawyer – says you can't do that!"

My stomach started to grumble. Vivi hadn't even been there and was talking nonsense! My arm immediately shot up to explain what had really happened, but Smelly Toes got there before me.

"Anyone who knows Mrs Owl knows what a kind-hearted person she is. I'm sure the last thing on her mind was to trick people into parting with their money. Unfortunately, I was unable to attend the event, but friends of mine had a great time dressing up."

I leaned back with a smile as Vivi shrank down in her chair with nothing else to say.

Leo, at my side, did have something to say. "I was there too, and it was great!" he declared. "So many characters from books – it was mad. And the idea of paying what you thought your book was worth was also fantastic."

Nino and Darius turned and glared at him. Reading was probably the last thing they did in their free time. Hopefully they weren't going to threaten Leo with a beating now.

"Really? You were there too?" I whispered. "I didn't see you."

"It was very busy, wasn't it?" he whispered back.

Nino and Darius turned back around, shaking their heads, and Ms Rose carried on talking. Huh? Did I just call her *Ms Rose*? That just slipped out!

"Before we start our topic for today, I'd like to collect in your diaries. If you want to, that is – as I explained before. But I'd be happy if you'd let me read your thoughts."

Did I just imagine it or did Ms Rose give me a particularly intense look? I suddenly wasn't so sure if I should hand in my glittery notebook. I was pretty angry when I wrote down everything that was upsetting me and maybe I'd written some things that weren't very nice. After all, she had just defended Mrs Owl and she seemed to have made an effort with Lottie. But then I remembered how sad Lottie was at the moment. And about how she was going to miss another great event at Mrs Owl's Bookshop. Defiantly, I pressed my notebook into Ms Rose's hand as she stood in front of me.

When she had walked around the classroom, she announced that we would spend this lesson talking about our favourite books – finally a topic that I enjoyed! I was even a bit disappointed when the bell rang for break, because Vivi went on about *Holly Polly's Perfect Pony* for so long that not everyone got a turn. I really wanted to hear what Leo's favourite book was and what he had come dressed up as on Saturday.

I strolled across the playground, with my sandwich in hand (liverwurst, of course), and sat down on the bench where Lottie and I often used to sit together and watch the older boys playing basketball. I'd just popped in the last mouthful when I heard a strange sound.

"*Pssst!*" I heard behind me. And again: "*Pssst!*"

I turned around, but all there was behind me were the fence and bushes on the edge of the playground. I once again turned my attention back to the basketball players. One of them had just scored.

"*Pssst*, Clara!" I heard again. And then: "Ooh, ouch!"

I stared at one of the bushes, which was now trembling suspiciously. Suddenly a hand emerged and grabbed at one of the fence posts. That was followed shortly after by a face.

"Lottie?" I gasped.

"Shhh, not so loud!" she whispered.

I jumped up and had no idea what to do. It couldn't be! How could Lottie possibly be here?

"Wow! OK, come on, I'll help you over the fence," I exclaimed enthusiastically, at which point Lottie's head vanished back into the bushes.

"Don't let anyone know that I'm here!" she whispered, and I could hardly hear her.

"What did you say?" I asked softly, kneeling very close to the fence. And then in surprise I whispered, "Did you run away?"

"Yes, kind of!" Lottie sounded a bit apologetic.

My heart started beating like crazy. "And now what do we do?"

"No idea!" came the answer from the bush.

"Look at this, Sarah!" I heard the vilest voice I knew. "Now Clara's so desperate she's started talking to the plants and bushes!"

I hadn't noticed Vivi. Without stopping to think about it, my hands gripped the fence and I pulled myself up high enough to get my right leg up and over the slats.

"Hey!" Vivi shouted so loud that no one could miss her. "What are you doing? We're not allowed to leave the playground!"

Now I had to hurry. "Run on ahead," I hissed to Lottie, and there came an almighty rustling from the bush.

I'd almost made it over the fence when Vivi grabbed my wrist.

"Stay here!" she screamed. "Ms Rose! Ms Rose! Clara's trying to run away!"

I tried to shake off Vivi, but she had a firm grip.

"Stop!" she shrieked as I released myself with one last tug.

I jumped over the fence and ran as fast as I could. Lottie was a few metres ahead. We turned into a side street and zigzagged between the houses until we stopped at a corner, out of breath.

"I don't think anybody followed us," I gasped. "And if they did, I think we've shaken them off our tail."

"Thank you," Lottie said, hugging me. "And hello!"

We stood there and had a huge hug, wheezing and laughing. It felt as good as a cup of hot chocolate with cream on a cold winter's day. Or that happy moment when you've finished reading a brilliant book.

"Did you really run away?" I finally asked.

"I couldn't take it any more," Lottie answered. "The kids in my class are so stupid and I just wanted to see you again and be with you tonight."

"Did you tell anyone?" I asked.

Lottie shook her head. "Mum would never have let me!"

"So what are we going to do?" I thought out loud. "Well, I guess there's one place where we're safe."

Lottie looked at me with a beaming smile. "The bookshop."

Fortunately, it wasn't far to the bookshop. We ran like the wind, and when we stepped through the door, it was as if we'd reached a safe harbour after a rough crossing. Nothing could happen to us here.

Mrs Owl was on a stepladder, humming to herself as she dusted the cobwebs away.

"Hello!" I said, unable to resist a grin. "I've brought someone with me!"

When Mrs Owl turned around, she almost fell off the ladder in surprise. "Lottie! That's wonderful!" She climbed down and hugged us. "What are you doing here? Well, never mind. Now sit down for a nice slice of chocolate cake!" She patted Gustaf's head. "Yes, I know you're rather peckish too. Maybe I'll find you a little something."

My gaze wandered first to Gustaf and then to Mrs Owl. Did he say something? Also, why had he forgotten to announce our arrival with a rhyme?

"Yes, I'm glad too!" Mrs Owl said to Mr King. "Thank you, I will." She smiled at Lottie. "Mr King is happy to see you again."

"Thanks," Lottie said.

Mrs Owl gave me a questioning look. "Are you OK, Clara?"

I suddenly felt really strange. "I can't hear Gustaf any more," I said quietly. "Or Mr King."

"What?" said Mrs Owl. "That can't be! Show me your hands."

I didn't know what my hands had to do with it, but I held them out for Mrs Owl.

"Where's your bracelet?" she asked, running her thumb over my palms.

I'd always worn my bracelet on my right wrist ever since Mrs Owl gave it to me, and usually I never took it off, but now it wasn't there!

"I don't know!" I said, feeling despair spread inside me. It was as though I'd lost my hearing, because without the chattering voices of Mr King and Gustaf, it felt eerily silent in Mrs Owl's shop.

Mrs Owl brought us all a slice of chocolate cake and we sat down on the carpet beneath the children's mezzanine.

"Don't worry, Clara," she said. "I'm sure you'll be able to hear them soon. Very sure. Trust me, OK? And now please don't sulk because today is..."

"Today's no day to be down in the dumps, I know," I added.

She was right. I should be happy that Lottie was here and not worry about something else. But why had Mrs Owl asked about the bracelet?

When I asked about it, she just waved it off.

"Never mind, just enjoy the nice afternoon with your friend. You can stay here as long as you want if you don't mind me tidying up a bit around you. There's still a lot to do before this evening."

I couldn't shake off the feeling that Mrs Owl was keeping something from me. But I was unlikely to find out more today. She had already jumped up and started dragging a box of books into her office.

"How wonderful, how wonderful," she whispered. "A reunion is the sweetest pleasure."

Before I could give another thought to the bracelet, the shop door flew open. Ms Rose came rushing in and right behind her was Lottie's dad Daniel.

"Quick, we have to hide," I said, but it was obvious that it was too late.

"Here you are!" exclaimed Ms Rose, breathless. "You really worried us!" She didn't sound cross when she said it but genuinely concerned.

"Lottie!" Daniel shouted and came bounding over to us. He scooped her up in his arms and squeezed her so hard that she probably couldn't breathe. "Never do that again, never – do you hear?"

I couldn't understand Lottie's answer because she was sobbing. Even her dad had a tear in his eye.

"Come on," said Mrs Owl, "we'd better leave them to it." She took my hand and pulled me over to Ms Rose.

"Next time, you can just let me know," she said to me. "Special rules apply in my class when you need to see your best friend again." Ms Rose smiled. "You can miss lessons and go to a bookshop, for example."

"Good to know," I said. And then I smiled too. This time it wasn't a forced smile but a genuine one.

"And this is yours, isn't it?" Ms Rose rummaged in her pocket and pulled out my bracelet.

I wanted to squeal and throw my arms around her. But of course I didn't.

"Thanks," I said, and Mrs Owl helped me to put the bracelet back on.

"This is my favourite kind of story," cried Mr King. "One with a happy ending!"

Ending? The story wasn't finished yet. But it was well on its way.

10

MOONLIGHT BOOK NIGHT

Half an hour later, my parents had arrived at the bookshop, Lottie's dad had called Lottie's mum and told her where their daughter was and that everything was OK, and Mrs Owl had gleefully clapped her hands and declared what a wonderful day it was. And so it was. The grown-ups agreed that Lottie could stay at mine all weekend. And we could go to the Moonlight Book Night together!

Mrs Owl threw us out at one point so she could finish her final preparations for the evening, but a few hours later, when it was getting dark, Mum, Dad, Lottie and I were back at the shop door.

When we stepped inside, the bookshop had a magical party atmosphere. There were candlelit lamps everywhere, giving off a warm cosy glow, and soft music in the background. The book display tables were gone and in their place were three buffet tables with glasses of tea lights on them and tomato and smoked salmon canapés. There was a small bar on the counter for guests to help themselves to a drink. My gaze wandered to the children's books corner, which also had a small buffet table. I went up and found the table laden with chocolate cake, cinnamon swirls and gummy bears. I had to smile because I could tell who had helped Mrs Owl choose this selection of goodies.

Everything looked beautiful and I had a warm, comfortable feeling inside. But the best surprise was hanging on the walls. Every single previously empty space was covered with photos of people in fancy dress – these were the photos Dad had taken last Saturday.

"You didn't tell me about that!" I said, laughing when I saw a picture of Grandma as a nurse talking to a Dr Bernhardt.

"An artist's secret," said Dad with a smile.

The shop was getting busy. Mrs Owl flitted between the bookshelves and her till, nodding in a friendly

way to her guests, pouring wine and sparkling water, and taking money, her face radiant all the while with a beaming smile.

"Can I buy one of these photos?" asked an elderly woman who had just spotted a picture of herself.

Mrs Owl gave Dad a questioning look.

What a brilliant idea, I thought. Why hadn't we come up with it ourselves? That would bring a little more money into the till. After all, Mrs Owl needed every penny she could get to make up for the damage Mr Schwartz had caused.

But I didn't expect Dad not to agree. "No!" he said. "These pictures are not for sale."

"What?" I exclaimed.

Dad laughed. "You can simply take your picture away with you but I would ask you to kindly make a donation in this piggy bank here – for the preservation of our bookshop!" He pointed to the porcelain pig that had been standing there since the fancy-dress event, waiting to be filled.

Mrs Owl's eyes began to shine. "Thank you," she whispered, so only Dad and I could hear.

"When it comes to supporting our bookshop, my

photo is worth fifty!" one man called out as he walked solemnly over to the piggy bank.

The other guests nodded in agreement and pulled notes of all sizes from their purses.

Mrs Owl was so touched that she had to wipe away a few tears. If everyone carried on feeding the piggy bank like this, the shop would be here for years to come.

"Friends, don't just stand around and dribble, everyone come and have a nibble!" Gustaf called cheerfully. "No better way to lift your mood than delicious snacks and party food!" he rhymed. "And, my dear Clara, what would you say...to sneaking me a little salmon canapé?"

"That greedy cat," I said to Lottie after my parents had disappeared behind a bookshelf. "He's after a canapé too!"

"All right!" Lottie said, bowing down to pass him one surreptitiously. "Too bad I can't understand him."

"Sometimes it's best that way, believe me," I said, stroking Gustaf's head.

"Hey, what's that supposed to mean?" he asked indignantly. "Just one," he added. "One is barely a step from none! Oh and I rather fancy a cinnamon bun and maybe some gummy bears for fun." He licked his paws and his tummy rumbled. "Mrs Owl wouldn't let me make an early start on tea – she doesn't want any more bad press, you see."

I picked up another canapé and dropped it unobtrusively under the table. "I'm sure there's no risk of that," I assured him.

Unlike Gustaf, I knew who the nice newspaper reporter was – the one Mrs Owl spoke to on the phone yesterday. It wasn't long before he came in the door.

"Dad!" Lottie shouted, waving to him.

Daniel, Lottie's father, was the editor of the local newspaper. Together with his companion – Ms Rose, of course – he made his way through the crowd of guests and joined us.

"Well, are you having a nice time?" asked Ms Rose. "I'd like to see what I can find for our class library. Maybe you could help me?"

"Yes, maybe," I said, squeezing Lottie's hand.

I knew that she still found it hard to talk to her dad's new girlfriend so I was all the more astonished when she said, "Maybe something about snakes. The others might find it interesting anyway." She giggled softly, and I couldn't help joining her.

"I see," said Ms Rose with a wink, and she told Daniel about my book tip for Lottie.

He laughed loudly. "I could have told you right away! Lottie was even scared of worms when she was little!" He put an arm around his daughter and together they walked over to one of the shelves.

Now I was alone with just Ms Rose Smelly Toes.

"Don't worry!" cried Mr King. "You're well on your way. Talk to her, get to know her. After all, the school year has just begun. Are you going to be angry with her all year until the next summer holiday?"

"I've read your diary," said Ms Rose, and I winced. "I'm so sorry you've gone through so much on my account," she went on. "I didn't want that. There's nothing worse than losing your best friend, I know. And I see how important you two are to each other." She took a sip from the glass of wine that Daniel had pressed into her hand. "I wish I could make amends but I don't know how." She looked at me as if I had to tell her.

Suddenly the shop door opened, and all conversation seemed to come to an abrupt halt.

"Get out! Shoo! Away with you!" Gustaf hissed, but of course the new guest couldn't understand him.

"What impudence!" cried Mr King. "To venture in here!"

A grin crossed my face. "I've got an idea of how you could make it up to me," I said to Ms Rose, nodding towards the door. "We'd like to get rid of that unwanted guest over there."

Ms Rose frowned for a moment as she thought, but then a sly smile spread over her face and she nodded.

Mr Schwartz greeted everyone solemnly, as if we had all been waiting for him. "Good evening, all," he said. "I was curious to see what's going on here." He confidently sauntered over to the bar.

"Welcome, welcome," muttered Mrs Owl, gesturing with a hand. "Every guest is welcome here. How lovely that you've come!"

I saw Mr Schwartz's mouth turn down at the corners. He hadn't expected such a friendly greeting.

Ms Rose strolled resolutely over to Mr Schwartz, who was pouring himself a glass of wine. She tapped him on the shoulder. "Excuse me," she said. "Would you be so kind?"

Mr Schwartz's eyes opened widely. "I'd be delighted!" he answered effusively. "Red or white?"

"Red please! A large one, if you would," she said.

Mr Schwartz grabbed the wine bottle and poured Ms Rose a large glass. Then he raised his own glass to toast with Ms Rose.

"May I introduce myself? I'm Erich!" he said, nodding his head grandly.

I started to feel queasy. What was Ms Rose doing talking to him?

"Sophie!" she said cheerfully, pretending to clink her glass against his. Instead she jolted the glass forward so that the entire glassful splashed on to Mr Schwartz's shirt.

Lottie clapped her hand over her mouth in surprise but couldn't stifle a loud laugh. I too could hardly restrain myself and burst out laughing.

Mr Schwartz looked down at the huge, red, wet patch and then glared at Ms Rose. "There'll be consequences..." he hissed. "For you and for the shop!"

"Oh sure, don't hold back," said Ms Rose.

"This is going to be a great article about the Moonlight Book Night," called Daniel as he approached, scribbling something in his notebook as he walked. "What was your name again? Mr Fartz, was it?"

"*You?*" said Mr Schwartz angrily. "Didn't you or one of your lousy colleagues promise me that an ad in your rag of a newspaper would have the desired effect?"

"Ah, so do you admit that you were the mysterious caller who posted the ad about Mrs Owl's Bookshop giving out free books?"

"I have nothing to confess!" roared Mr Schwartz angrily.

"Well, well!" exclaimed Mrs Owl, clapping her hands. "Today's no day to be down in the dumps!"

"I'll report you to the police for disturbing the peace out of hours," Mr Schwartz went on. "And for misleading advertising. And for contravening shop opening rules!"

Suddenly a plump man raised his hand. "I'm a police officer by the way," he said. "I'd love to help you, sir, but unfortunately I'm not on duty. And besides, I don't see any cause for complaint here."

Mr Schwartz could do no more than give an insulted grunt.

"Friedrich, would you mind taking a few pictures of the event?" Lottie's dad asked mine, rubbing his hands together happily.

"Gladly!" answered Dad.

When he headed in Mr Schwartz's direction with his camera, the unwelcome guest turned on his heel to leave.

"There will be consequences," he snarled again as he left the shop.

"He won't be back," said Mr King. "Now we can celebrate in peace."

"Well, I'm feeling much better now," I mumbled softly to myself.

"Why's that?" asked Ms Rose, who was standing next to me again.

I thought for a moment then I looked at her with a grin. "Because you got rid of that old Fart Schwartz!"

Ms Rose smiled and held out her hand. "So, we've made our peace?"

"Yes," I said, shaking it.

The rest of the evening went without further incident. People drank wine, ate nibbles, leafed through the books, bought books and fed the piggy bank on the way. Just as Mrs Owl had hoped. Even better, in fact. She beamed as she sashayed around the shop, stopping occasionally to give Mr King's frame a stroke or whisper something into Gustaf's ear. Here and there a few of the names and images from the covers and spines of the books came and sat on the edge of the shelves, making themselves comfortable where they could observe the comings and goings in the shop. But they behaved themselves and anyone who didn't know better would have thought they were just decorations.

The shop door opened again. *Oh no – is Mr Schwartz back?*

But when I saw who came in, my heart skipped a beat. It was Velda, the vampire princess from last Saturday!

She was wearing the wig again, but when I looked at her face closer up, she seemed familiar.

"Oh," cried Mrs Owl. "How wonderful that you've dressed up! Welcome, Velda!"

The vampire princess bowed briefly and then headed in my direction.

"Well, this is a lovely surprise!" said Ms Rose.

No! It couldn't be!

Here she was, Velda – someone who I'd hoped might become my

new friend. Velda, who vanished suddenly on Saturday during the fancy-dress event, although I would have loved to talk to her. But the vampire princess wasn't a girl at all. Velda was...

"Bit thrown off, eh?" said Leo, his grin widening.

"B-but...you're..." I stammered.

"A boy?" he said. "Well, it's not just girls who love Velda. It's also my favourite book!"

My head was spinning, but Mr King brought my thoughts back into focus.

"So your new girlfriend is a male friend after all?" he chuckled.

I thought of how Leo had helped me with Podge and how he came up with an excuse when I was late to school. How nice he had been to me during PE and how he gave me chocolate when I should have been giving *him* a present to say sorry for his injured ankle. Only friends did that kind of thing, I realised.

I looked from Leo up to Lottie and back again.

"Yes," I said finally to Mr King, "it looks like it!"

"Well, it's worth a try," the mirror encouraged me.

I grinned at Leo and he grinned back.

"Come on, let me introduce you to someone!" I said.

We went up to the children's mezzanine, where Lottie was looking at a book.

I tapped her on the shoulder. "Look who's here. Leo, my new desk mate."

She turned and smiled. "Hello, I'm Lottie. I've heard lots about you."

"All good things, of course," I said quickly, though that was only half true. But Leo didn't need to know that.

The rest of the evening, Lottie, Leo and I sat on the beanbags and read to each other from our favourite books. I was happier than I'd been in a very long time.

"Good friends are like a cinnamon bun," said Gustaf, leaping up on to my lap. "You can always do with more than one."

That was probably another of his Swedish proverbs. And I had to agree.

THE AUTHOR

Katja Frixe studied education and worked for several years as an editor at various publishers of children's and young adult books before she became self-employed as a writer and translator. She lives with her husband and twin daughters in Braunschweig, Germany.

THE ILLUSTRATOR

Florentine Prechtel studied classical painting and sculpture in Mönchengladbach, Karlsruhe and Freiburg. After some exciting artistic projects in Berlin, Barcelona and Rome, she switched to illustrating children's books. She lives with her family in Freiburg im Breisgau, Germany.

THE TRANSLATOR

Ruth Ahmedzai Kemp is a British translator of fiction and non-fiction from German, Russian and Arabic. She lives with her husband and two boys in Cheltenham, England.

PRE-READING QUESTIONS:

1. The bookshop is the central setting of this story. Is there a bookshop near you? How often do you go and how important is it to you?

2. This is a book about friends and how friendships change. Can you think of a time where your friendship with someone changed? How hard do you think it is to make new friends?

3. Families can play a very important role in how we keep up friendships. Do you think there can sometimes be conflict between your family and your friends? How do you think this can be resolved?

QUESTIONS FOR DISCUSSION:

1. Have you ever had to say goodbye to someone? How does Katja Frixe capture that feeling?

2. Early on in the story, Clara's family are described as always being "there for each other". How is this shown throughout the book?

3. Why do you think Leo is nice to Clara? Do you think Clara understands him well?

4. How does Clara's attitude towards Sophie Rose change by the end of the story? What moments are important in changing Clara's mind?

5. We learn that not everyone can understand Gustaf and Mr King. How do you think the story would be different if everyone could? What role do they play in Clara's life?

6. Do books play a role in how friendships are made in the story?

7. What does Mrs Owl mean to Clara? Do you think she is a friend?

8. At the end of the story, Lottie, Leo and Clara all sit together and read. Do you think Leo will also become Lottie's friend?

9. Ms Rose says "There's nothing worse than losing your best friend." Do you agree? Do you think Clara has lost Lottie?

10. Why do you think Mrs Owl gives others chocolate cake? How do the characters feel when they are eating it? What does it tell us about Mrs Owl?

POST-READING ACTIVITIES

1. The magical bookshop is an important place for the village community: it is where they come together and find help for their problems, but it is also frequently in danger of closing. Think of a place in your community that provides a space for

people to come together. Write a fundraising ad for it.

2. The story is narrated by Clara who writes in her friendship book regularly about the activities she does and the new friends she makes. We learn that Lottie is struggling to make friends and feels lonely. Write an entry in Lottie's friendship book, after Clara told her about the magical bookshop's costume party.

3. Find or invent a chocolate cake recipe that "always lifts the spirits". Have a go at baking it with a friend or parent!

4. Think about your favourite book. Find out as much as you can about the author and make a poster. Ask your class if anyone else likes the book.

5. Organise a reading group about a book that you and a friend both like. See if you can hold it in a library or local bookshop.

JOIN OUR CONVERSATION ONLINE!

Follow us for a behind-the-scenes look at our books.

There'll be news, exclusive content and giveaways galore!

@rocktheboatnews
oneworld-publications.com/rtb

ROCK THE BOAT